Frances Hodgson Burnett

Louisiana

Frances Hodgson Burnett

Louisiana

ISBN/EAN: 9783743367715

Manufactured in Europe, USA, Canada, Australia, Japa

Cover: Foto ©Andreas Hilbeck / pixelio.de

Manufactured and distributed by brebook publishing software (www.brebook.com)

Frances Hodgson Burnett

Louisiana

"ASK YOUR SISTER," SHE REPLIED. "IT WAS HER PLAN."

(*Page 80.*)

BY

FRANCES HODGSON BURNETT

AUTHOR OF "HAWORTH'S" "THAT LASS O' LOWRIE'S," ETC.

NEW YORK

CHARLES SCRIBNER'S SONS

743 AND 745 BROADWAY

1880

TROW'S
PRINTING AND BOOKBINDING CO.,
201–213 *East 12th St.*,
NEW YORK.

CONTENTS.

LOUISIANA.

CHAPTER I.

LOUISIANA.

OLIVIA FERROL leaned back in her chair, her hands folded upon her lap. People passed and repassed her as they promenaded the long "gallery," as it was called; they passed in couples, in trios; they talked with unnecessary loudness, they laughed at their own and each other's jokes; they flirted, they sentimentalized, they criticised each other, but none of them showed any special interest in Olivia Ferrol, nor did Miss Ferrol, on her part, show much interest in them.

She had been at Oakvale Springs for two weeks. She was alone, out of her element, and knew nobody. The fact that she was a New Yorker, and had never before been so far South, was rather against her. On her arrival she had been glanced over and commented upon with candor.

1

"She is a Yankee," said the pretty and re-
markably youthful-looking mother of an apparently grown-up family from New Orleans. "You
can see it."   -

And though the remark was not meant to be
exactly severe, Olivia felt that it was very severe,
indeed, under existing circumstances. She heard
it as she was giving her orders for breakfast to
her own particular jet-black and highly excitable
waiter, and she felt guilty at once and blushed,
hastily taking a sip of ice-water to conceal her
confusion. When she went upstairs afterward she
wrote a very interesting letter to her brother in
New York, and tried to make an analysis of her
sentiments for his edification.

"You advised me to come here because it
would be novel as well as beneficial," she wrote.
"And it certainly is novel. I think I feel like a
Pariah—a little. I am aware that even the best
bred and most intelligent of them, hearing that I
have always lived in New York, will privately regret it if they like me and remember it if they
dislike me. Good-natured and warm-hearted as
they seem among themselves, I am sure it will be
I who will have to make the advances—if advances are made—and I must be very amiable,
indeed, if I intend that they shall like me."

But she had not been well enough at first to be in the humor to make the advances, and consequently had not found her position an exciting one. She had looked on until **she had** been able to rouse herself **to some pretty** active likes **and** dislikes, **but she knew no one.**

She felt this afternoon as if this mild **recreation of looking on had begun** rather to pall upon her, **and she** drew out her watch, glancing at it with a little yawn.

" It is five o'clock," she said. " Very soon the band will make its appearance, **and it** will bray until the stages come in. Yes, there it is !"

The musical combination to which she referred **was composed of** six or seven gentlemen **of** color **who played upon brazen instruments, each in different keys and** different **time.** Three times a day they collected **on** a rustic kiosk upon the lawn and played divers popular airs with an intensity, fervor, and muscular power worthy of a better cause. They straggled up as she spoke, took their places and began, and before they had played many minutes the most exciting event of the day **occurred, as it always did** somewhere about this **hour.** In the midst of the gem of their collection **was** heard the rattle **of** wheels **and** the crack of **whips, and** through the rapturous shouts of the juvenile guests, the two venerable, rickety stages dashed up with a lumbering flourish, and a spasmodic pretense of excitement, calculated to deceive only the feeblest mind.

At the end of the gallery they checked themselves in their mad career, the drivers making strenuous efforts to restrain the impetuosity of the four steeds whose harness rattled against their ribs with an unpleasant bony sound. Half a dozen waiters rushed forward, the doors were flung open, the steps let down with a bang, the band brayed insanely, and the passengers alighted. —" One, two, three, four," counted Olivia Ferrol, mechanically, as the first vehicle unburdened itself. And then, as the door of the second was opened : " One—only one : and a very young one, too. Dear me ! Poor girl !"

This exclamation might naturally have fallen from any quick-sighted and sympathetic person. The solitary passenger of the second stage stood among the crowd, hesitating, and plainly overwhelmed with timorousness. Three waiters were wrestling with an ugly shawl, a dreadful shining valise, and a painted wooden trunk, such as is seen in country stores. In their enthusiastic desire to dispose creditably of these articles they temporarily forgot the owner, who, after one desperate, timid glance at them, looked round her in vain **for** succor. She was very pretty and **very** young and very ill-dressed—her costume a bucolic travesty on prevailing modes. **She did not** know where to go, and **no one thought of showing her ;** the loungers **about the office stared at her ;** she **began to turn pale with** embarrassment and timidity. **Olivia Ferrol** left her chair **and** crossed the **gallery.** She spoke to a servant a little sharply :

" Why not show the young lady into the parlor ? " she said.

The girl heard, and looked at her helplessly, but with gratitude. The waiter **darted forward** with hospitable rapture.

. **" Dis yeah's de way, miss,"** he said, " right **inter de 'ception-room. Foller me, ma'am."**

Olivia returned to her seat. People were re-garding her with **curiosity,** but **she was** entirely oblivious of the fact.

" That is one of them," she was saying, mentally. " That is one of them, and a very interesting type it is, too."

' To render the peculiarities of this young woman **clearer, it may** be well to reveal here something **of her** past life **and surroundings. Her** father **had been a** literary man, her mother an illustrator of books and magazine articles. From her earliest childhood she had been surrounded by men and women of artistic or literary occupations, some who were drudges, some who were geniuses, some who balanced between the two extremes, and she had unconsciously learned the tricks of the trade. She had been used to people who continually had their eyes open to anything peculiar and interesting in human nature, who were enraptured by the discovery of new types of men, women, and emotions. Since she had been left an orphan she had lived with her brother, who had been reporter, editor, contributor, critic, one after the other, until at last he had established a very enviable reputation as a brilliant, practical young fellow, who knew his business, and had a fine career open to him. So it was natural that, having become interested in the general friendly fashion of dissecting and studying every scrap of human nature within reach, she had followed more illustrious examples, and had become very critical upon the subject of "types" herself. During her sojourn at Oakvale she had studied the North Carolinian mountaineer "type" with the enthusiasm of an amateur. She had talked to the women in sunbonnets who brought fruit to the hotel, and sat on the steps and floor of the galleries awaiting the advent of customers with a composure only to be equaled by the calmness of the noble savage; she had walked and driven over the mountain roads, stopping at wayside houses and entering into conversation with the owners until **she had become** comparatively well known, **even in the space of a fortnight, and** she had **taken notes for her** brother **until** she had **roused him to sharing her** own **interest in her** discoveries.

" I am sure you will find a great deal of material here," she wrote to him. " You see how I have fallen a victim to that dreadful habit of looking at everything in **the** light **of** material. A man is **no** longer **a** man—he **is** ' material '; **sorrow** is not sorrow, joy is not joy—it is ' material.' There is something **rather ghoulish in it. I** wonder **if anatomists look at people's bodies as** we **do at** their **minds, and if to them** every **one is a** ' subject.' **At** present **I** am interested in a species of girl I have discovered. Sometimes she belongs to the better class—the farmers, who have a great deal of land and who are the rich men of the community,—sometimes she lives **in a log** cabin with a **mother** who **smokes and chews** tobacco, **but** in either **case** she is a surprise **and a** mystery. She **is** always pretty, she **is** occasionally beautiful, and **in** spite of her house, her people, her education or want of it, she is instinctively a refined and delicately susceptible young person. She has always been to some common school, where she has written compositions on sentimental or touching subjects, and when she belongs to the better class she takes a fashion magazine and tries to make her dresses like those of the ladies in the colored plates, and, I may add, frequently fails. I could write a volume about her, but I wont. When your vacation arrives, come and see for yourself."

It was of this class Miss Ferrol was thinking when she said : '' That is one of them, and a very intering type it is, too."

When she went in to the dining-room to partake of the six o'clock supper, she glanced about her in search of the new arrival, but she had not yet appeared. A few minutes later, however, she entered. She came in slowly, looking straight before her, and trying very hard to appear at ease. She was prettier than before, and worse dressed. She wore a blue, much-ruffled muslin and a wide collar made of imitation lace. She had tucked her sleeves up to her elbow with a band and bow of black velvet, and her round, smooth young arms were adorable. She looked for a vacant place, and, seeing none, stopped short, as if she did not know what to do. Then some magnetic attraction drew her eye to Olivia Ferrol's. After a moment's pause, she moved timidly toward her.

" I—I wish a waiter would come," she faltered.

At that moment one on the wing stopped in obedience to a gesture of Miss Ferrol's—a delicate, authoritative movement of the head.

" Give this young lady that chair opposite me," she said.

The chair was drawn out with a flourish, the girl was seated, and the bill of fare was placed in her hands.

" Thank you," she said, in a low, astonished voice.

Olivia smiled.

" That waiter is my own special and peculiar property," she said, " and I rather pride myself on him."

But her guest scarcely seemed to comprehend her pleasantry. She looked somewhat awkward.

" I—don't know much about waiters," she ventured. " I'm not used to them, and I suppose they know it. I never was at a hotel before."

" You will soon get used to them," returned Miss Ferrol.

The girl fixed her eyes upon her with a ques-

1*

tioning appeal. They were the loveliest eyes she had ever seen, Miss Ferrol thought—large-irised, and with wonderful long lashes fringing them and curling upward, giving them a tender, very wide-open look. She seemed suddenly to gain courage, and also to feel it her duty to account for herself.

" I shouldn't have come here alone if I could have got father to come with me," she revealed. " But he wouldn't come. He said it wasn't the place for him. I haven't been very well since mother died, and he thought I'd better try the Springs awhile. I don't think I shall like it."

" I don't like it," replied Miss Ferrol, candidly, " but I dare say you will when you know people."

The girl glanced rapidly and furtively over the crowded room, and then her eyes fell.

" I shall never know them," she said, in a depressed undertone.

In secret Miss Ferrol felt a conviction that she was right ; she had not been presented under the right auspices.

" It is rather clever and sensitive in her to find it out so quickly," she thought. " Some girls would be more sanguine, and be led into blunders."

They progressed pretty well during the meal.

When it was over, and Miss Ferrol rose, she became conscious that her companion was troubled by some new difficulty, and a second thought suggested to her what its nature was.

"Are you going to your room?" she asked.

"I don't know," said the girl, with the look of helpless appeal again. "I don't know where else to go. I don't like to go out there" (signifying the gallery) "alone."

"Why not come with me?" said Miss Ferrol. "Then we can promenade together."

"Ah!" she said, with a little gasp of relief and gratitude. "Don't you mind?"

"On the contrary, I shall be very glad of your society," Miss Ferrol answered. "I am alone, too."

So they went out together and wandered slowly from one end of the starlit gallery to the other, winding their way through the crowd that promenaded, and, upon the whole, finding it rather pleasant.

"I shall have to take care of her," Miss Ferrol was deciding; "but I do not think I shall mind the trouble."

The thing that touched her most was the girl's innocent trust in her sincerity—her taking for granted that this stranger, who had been polite to her, had been so not for worldly good breeding's sake, but from true friendliness and extreme generosity of nature. Her first shyness conquered, she related her whole history with the unreserve of a child. Her father was a farmer, and she had always lived with him on his farm. He had been too fond of her to allow her to leave home, and she had never been " away to school."

" He has made a pet of me at home," she said. " I was the only one that lived to be over eight years old. I am the eleventh. Ten died before I was born, and it made father and mother worry a good deal over me—and father was worse than mother. He said the time never seemed to come when he could spare me. He is very good and kind —is father," she added, in a hurried, soft-voiced way. " He's rough, but he's very good and kind."

Before they parted for the night Miss Ferrol had the whole genealogical tree by heart. They were an amazingly prolific family, it seemed. There was Uncle Josiah, who had ten children, Uncle Leander, who had fifteen, Aunt Amanda, who had twelve, and Aunt Nervy, whose belongings comprised three sets of twins and an unlimited supply of odd numbers. They went upstairs together and parted at Miss Ferrol's door, their rooms being near each other.

The girl held out her hand.

"Good-night!" she said. "I'm so thankful I've got to know you."

Her eyes looked bigger and wider-open than ever; she smiled, showing her even, sound, little white teeth. Under the bright light of the lamp the freckles the day betrayed on her smooth skin were not to be seen.

"Dear me!" thought Miss Ferrol. "How startlingly pretty, in spite of the cotton lace and the dreadful polonaise!"

She touched her lightly on the shoulder.

"Why, you are as tall as I am!" she said.

"Yes," the girl replied, depressedly; "but I'm twice as broad."

"Oh no—no such thing." And then, with a delicate glance down over her, she said—"It is your dress that makes you fancy so. Perhaps your dressmaker does not understand your fig-ure,"—as if such a failing was the most natural and simple thing in the world, and needed only the slightest rectifying.

"I have no dressmaker," the girl answered. "I make my things myself. Perhaps that is it."

"It is a little dangerous, it is true," replied Miss Ferrol. "I have been bold enough to try it myself, and I never succeeded. I could give you the address of a very thorough woman if you lived in New York."

" But I don't live there, you see.   I wish I did. I never shall, though.   Father could never spare me."

Another slight pause ensued, during which she looked admiringly at Miss Ferrol.   Then she said " good-night " again, and turned away.

But before she had crossed the corridor she stopped.

" I never told you my name," she said.

Miss Ferrol naturally expected she would announce it at once, but she did not.   An air of embarrassment fell upon her.   She seemed almost averse to speaking.

" Well," said Miss Ferrol, smiling, " what is it ? "

She did not raise her eyes from the carpet as she replied, unsteadily :

" It's Louisiana."

Miss Ferrol answered her very composedly :

" The name of the state ? "

" Yes.   Father came from there."

" But you did not tell me your surname."

" Oh ! that is Rogers.   You—you didn't laugh. I thought you would."

" At the first name ? " replied Miss Ferrol.

" Oh no. It is unusual—but names often are. And Louise is pretty."

"So it is," she said, brightening. " I never thought of that. I hate Louisa. They will call it ' Lowizy,' or ' Lousyanny.' I could sign my-self Louise, couldn't I ? "

" Yes," Miss Ferrol replied.

And then her *protégée* said " good-night " for the third time, and disappeared.

CHAPTER II.

WORTH.

SHE presented herself at the bed-room door with a timid knock the next morning before breakfast, evidently expecting to be taken charge of. Miss Ferrol felt sure she would appear, and had, indeed, dressed herself in momentary expectation of hearing the knock.

When she heard it she opened the door at once.

"I am glad to see you," she said. "I thought you might come."

A slight expression of surprise showed itself in the girl's eyes. It had never occurred to her that she might not come.

"Oh, yes," she replied. "I never could go down alone when there was any one who would go with me."

There was something on her mind, Miss Ferrol fancied, and presently it burst forth in a confidential inquiry.

"Is this dress very short-waisted?" she asked, with great earnestness.

Merciful delicacy stood in the way of Miss Ferrol's telling her how short-waisted it was, and how it maltreated her beautiful young body.

"It is rather short-waisted, it is true."

"Perhaps," the girl went on, with a touch of guileless melancholy, "I am naturally this shape."

Here, it must be confessed, Miss Ferrol forgot herself for the moment, and expressed her indignation with undue fervor.

"Perish the thought!" she exclaimed. "Why, child! your figure is a hundred times better than mine."

Louisiana wore for a moment a look of absolute fright.

"Oh, no!" she cried. "Oh, no. Your figure is magnificent."

"Magnificent!" echoed Miss Ferrol, giving way to her enthusiasm, and indulging in figures of speech. "Don't you see that I am thin—absolutely thin. But my things fit me, and my dressmaker understands me. If you were dressed as I am,"—pausing to look her over from head to foot—"Ah!" she exclaimed, pathetically, "how I should like to see you in some of my clothes!"

A tender chord was touched. A gentle sadness, aroused by this instance of wasted opportunities, rested upon her. But instantaneously she brightened, seemingly without any particular cause. A brilliant idea had occurred to her. But she did not reveal it.

"I will wait," she thought, "until she is more at her ease with me."

She really was more at her ease already. Just this one little scrap of conversation had done that. She became almost affectionate in a shy way before they reached the dining-room.

"I want to ask you something," she said, as they neared the door.

"What is it?"

She held Miss Ferrol back with a light clasp on her arm. Her air was quite tragic in a small way.

"Please say 'Louise,' when you speak to me," she said. "Never say 'Miss Louisiana'—never —never!"

"No, I shall never say 'Miss Louisiana,'" her companion answered. "How would you like 'Miss Rogers?'"

"I would rather have 'Louise,'" she said, disappointedly.

"Well," returned Miss Ferrol, "'Louise' let it be."

And "Louise" it was thenceforward. If she

had not been so pretty, so innocent, and so affectionate and humble a young creature, she might
have been troublesome **at** times (it occurred **to**
Olivia Ferrol), she clung so pertinaciously **to**
their chance acquaintanceship ; **she** was so helpless and **desolate if left to** herself, **and** so inordi-
nately **glad to be taken in** hand again.   **She made
no new friends,—which** was perhaps natural
enough, after all.   She had nothing in common
with the young women who played ten-pins and
croquet and rode out in parties with their cav-
aliers.   She was not of them, and understood
them as little as they understood her.   She knew
very well that they **regarded her** with scornful **tol-**
erance **when** they were **of the** ill-natured class,
and with ill-subdued wonder when they were
amiable.   She could not play ten-pins or croquet,
nor could she dance.

"What are the men kneeling down for, and
why do they keep stopping to put on those queer
little caps and things?" she whispered to Miss
Ferrol one night.

"They are trying **to dance a** German," replied
Miss Ferrol, "and the man who is leading them
only **knows** one figure."

As for the riding, she had been used to riding
all her life ; but no one asked her to join them,

and if they had done so she would have been too wise,—unsophisticated as she was,—to accept the invitation. So where Miss Ferrol was seen she was seen also, and she was never so happy as when she was invited into her protector's room and allowed to spend the morning or evening there. She would have been content to sit there forever and listen to Miss Ferrol's graphic description of life in the great world. The names of celebrated personages made small impression upon her. It was revealed gradually to Miss Ferrol that she had private doubts as to the actual existence of some of them, and the rest she had never heard of before.

"You never read 'The Scarlet Letter?'" asked her instructress upon one occasion.

She flushed guiltily.

"No," she answered. "Nor—nor any of the others."

Miss Ferrol gazed at her silently for a few moments. Then she asked her a question in a low voice, specially mellowed, so that it might not alarm her.

"Do you know who John Stuart Mill is?" she said.

"No," she replied from the dust of humiliation.

" Have you never heard—just *heard*—of Ruskin ? "

" **No.**"

" Nor of Michael **Angelo ? "**

" N-no—ye-es, I think so—perhaps, but I don't
know what he did."

" Do you," she continued, very slowly, " do—
you—know—anything—about—Worth ? "

" **No,** nothing."

Her questioner clasped her hands with repressed
emotion.

" Oh," she cried, " how—how you **have** been
neglected ! "

She was really depressed, but **her** *protégée* was
so much more deeply so that she felt it her duty
to contain herself and return to cheerfulness.

" Never mind," she said. " I will tell you
all I know about them, and,"—after a pause for
speculative thought upon the subject,—" by-the-
by, it isn't much, and I will lend you some
books to read, and give you a list of some you
must persuade your father to buy for you, **and**
you **will** be all right. It is rather dreadful **not**
to know the names **of** people **and things ; but,**
after **all, I** think there are very few people who—
ahem ! "

She was checked here by rigid conscientious

scruples. If she was to train this young mind in
the path of learning and literature, she must place
before her a higher standard of merit than the
somewhat shady and slipshod one her eagerness
had almost betrayed her into upholding. She had
heard people talk of "standards" and "ideals,"
and when she was kept to the point and in regu-
lation working order, she could be very eloquent
upon these subjects herself.

"You will have to work very seriously," she
remarked, rather incongruously and with a rapid
change of position. "If you wish to—to acquire
anything, you must read conscientiously and—and
with a purpose." She was rather proud of that
last clause.

"Must I?" inquired Louise, humbly. "I
should like to—if I knew where to begin. Who
was Worth? Was he a poet?"

Miss Ferrol acquired a fine, high color very
suddenly.

"Oh," she answered, with some uneasiness,
"you—you have no need to begin with Worth.
He doesn't matter so much—really."

"I thought," Miss Rogers said meekly, "that
you were more troubled about my not having read
what he wrote, than about my not knowing any
of the others."

"Oh, no. You see—the fact is, he—he never wrote anything."

"What did he do?" she asked, anxious for **in-**formation.

"He—it isn't **'did,' it is 'does.'** He—makes dresses."

"Dresses!"

This single word, but no exclamation point **could** express its tone of wild amazement.

"Yes."

"A man!"

"Yes."

There was a dead silence. **It was** embarrassing at first. Then the amazement of the unsophisticated one began to calm itself; it gradually **died down, and became another emot**ion, merging **itself into interest.**

"Does"—**guilelessly she** inquired—"he make nice ones?"

"Nice!" echoed Miss Ferrol. "They are works of art! I have got three in my trunk."

"O-o-h!" sighed Louisiana. "Oh, dear!"

Miss Ferrol rose from her chair.

"I will **show** them to you," she said. **"I—I** should like you to try them on."

"To try them on!" ejaculated the child in an awe-stricken tone. "Me?"

"Yes," said Miss Ferrol, unlocking the trunk and throwing back the lid. "I have been wanting to see you in them since the first day you came."

She took them out and laid them upon the bed on their trays. Louise got up from the floor and approaching, reverently stood near them. There was a cream-colored evening-dress of soft, thick, close-clinging silk of some antique-modern sort; it had golden fringe, and golden flowers embroidered upon it.

"Look at that," said Miss Ferrol, softly—even religiously.

She made a mysterious, majestic gesture.

"Come here," she said. "You must put it on."

Louise shrank back a pace.

"I—oh! I daren't," she cried. "It is too beautiful!"

"Come here," repeated Miss Ferrol.

She obeyed timorously, and gave herself into the hands of her controller. She was so timid and excited that she trembled all the time her toilette was being performed for her. Miss Ferrol went through this service with the manner of a priestess officiating at an altar. She laced up the back of the dress with the slender, golden cords;

she arranged the antique drapery which wound itself around in close swathing folds. There was not the shadow of a wrinkle from shoulder to hem: the lovely young figure was revealed in all its beauty of outline. There were no sleeves at all, there was not very much bodice, but there was a great deal of effect, and this, it is to be supposed, was the object.

"Walk across the floor," commanded Miss Ferrol.

Louisiana obeyed her.

"Do it again," said Miss Ferrol.

Having been obeyed for the second time, her hands fell together. Her attitude and expression could be said to be significant only of rapture.

"I said so!" she cried. "I said so! You might have been born in New York!"

It was a grand climax. Louisiana felt it to the depths of her reverent young heart. But she could not believe it. She was sure that it was too sublime to be true. She shook her head in deprecation.

"It is no exaggeration," said Miss Ferrol, with renewed fervor. "Laurence himself, if he were not told that you had lived here, would never guess it. I should like to try you on him."

2

"Who—is he?" inquired Louisiana. "Is he a writer, too?"

"Well, yes,—but not exactly like the others. He is my brother."

It was two hours before this episode ended. Only at the sounding of the second bell did Louisiana escape to her room to prepare for dinner.

Miss Ferrol began to replace the dresses in her trunk. She performed her task in an abstracted mood. When she had completed it she stood upright and paused a moment, with quite a startled air.

"Dear me!" she exclaimed. "I—actually forgot about Ruskin!"

CHAPTER III.

"HE IS DIFFERENT."

THE same evening, as they sat on one of the seats upon the lawn, Miss Ferrol became aware several times that Louisiana was regarding her with more than ordinary interest. She sat with her hands folded upon her lap, her eyes fixed on her face, and her pretty mouth actually a little open.

"What are you thinking of?" Olivia asked, at length.

The girl started, and recovered herself with an effort.

"I—well, I was thinking about—authors," she stammered.

"Any particular author?" inquired Olivia, "or authors as a class?"

"About your brother being one. I never thought I should see any one who knew an author —and you are related to one!"

Her companion's smile was significant of immense experience. It was plain that she was so accustomed to living on terms of intimacy with any number of authors that she could afford to feel indifferent about them.

" My dear," she said, amiably, " they are not in the least different from other people."

It sounded something like blasphemy.

" Not different !" cried Louisiana. " Oh, surely, they must be ! Isn't—isn't your brother different ? "

Miss Ferrol stopped to think. She was very fond of her brother. Privately she considered him the literary man of his day. She was simply disgusted when she heard experienced critics only calling him " clever " and " brilliant " instead of " great " and " world-moving."

" Yes," she replied at length, " he is different."

" I thought he must be," said Louisiana, with a sigh of relief. " You are, you know."

" Am I ?" returned Olivia. " Thank you. But I am not an author—at least,"—she added, guiltily, " nothing I have written has ever been published."

" Oh, why not ? " exclaimed Louisiana.

" Why not ? " she repeated, dubiously and thoughtfully. And then, knitting her brows, she said, " I don't know why not."

" I am sure if you have ever written anything, it ought to have been published," protested her adorer.

" *I* thought so," said Miss Ferrol. " But—but *they* didn't."

" They ? " echoed Louisiana. " Who are ' they ? ' "

" The editors," she replied, in a rather gloomy manner. " There is a great deal of wire-pulling, and favoritism, and—even envy and malice, of which those outside know nothing. You wouldn't understand it if I should tell you about it."

For a few moments she wore quite a fell expression, and gloom reigned. She gave her head a little shake.

" They regret it afterward," she remarked,— " frequently."

From which Louisiana gathered that it was the editors who were so overwhelmed, and she could not help sympathizing with them in secret. There was something in the picture of their unavailing remorse which touched her, despite her knowledge of the patent fact that they deserved it and could expect nothing better. She was quite glad when Olivia brightened up, as she did presently.

" Laurence is handsomer than most of them,

and has a more distinguished air," she said. "He is very charming. People always say so."

"I wish I could see him," ventured Louisiana.

"You will see him if you stay here much longer," replied Miss Ferrol. "It is quite likely he will come to Oakvale."

For a moment Louisiana fluttered and turned pale with pleasure, but as suddenly she drooped.

"I forgot," she faltered. "You will have to be with him always, and I shall have no one. He won't want me."

Olivia sat and looked at her with deepening interest. She was thinking again of a certain whimsical idea which had beset her several times since she had attired her *protégée* in the cream-colored robe.

"Louise," she said, in a low, mysterious tone, "how would you like to wear dresses like mine all the rest of the time you are here?"

The child stared at her blankly.

"I haven't got any," she gasped.

"No," said Miss Ferrol, with deliberation, "but *I* have."

She rose from her seat, dropping her mysterious air and smiling encouragingly.

"Come with me to my room," she said. "I want to talk to you."

If she had ordered her to follow her to the stake it is not at all unlikely that Louisiana would have obeyed. She got up meekly, smiling, too, and feeling sure something **very interesting** was going to happen. **She did not understand in the least,** but she was **quite tractable. And after they had reached the room and shut** themselves in, **she found that it** *was* **something very** interesting which **was to** happen.

"You remember what I said to you this morning?" Miss Ferrol suggested.

"You said so many things."

"Oh, but you cannot have forgotten this **partic- ular** thing. I said **you looked as if you** had **been** born **in New York."**

Louisiana remembered with a glow of rapture.

"Oh, yes," she answered.

"And I said Laurence himself would not know, if he **was not told, that you had** lived all your life here." ·

"Yes."

"And I said I should like to try you on him."

"Yes."

Miss **Ferrol** kept her eyes fixed **on her and** watched her closely.

"I have been **thinking of it** all the morning," she added. "I should like to try you **on** him."

Louisiana was silent a moment. Then she spoke, hesitatingly :

" Do you mean that I should pretend——," she began.

" Oh, no," interrupted Miss Ferrol. " Not pretend either one thing or the other. Only let me dress you as I choose, and then take care that you say nothing whatever about your past life. You will have to be rather quiet, perhaps, and let him talk. He will like that, of course—men always do—and then you will learn a great many things from him."

" It will be—a very strange thing to do," said Louisiana.

" It will be a very interesting thing," answered Olivia, her enthusiasm increasing. " How he will admire you ! "

Louisiana indulged in one of her blushes.

" Have you a picture of him ? "

" Yes. Why ? " she asked, in some surprise.

" Because I should like to see his face."

" Do you think," Miss Ferrol said, in further bewilderment, " that you might not like him ? "

" I think he might not like me."

" Not like you ! " cried Miss Ferrol. " You ! He will think you are divine—when you are dressed as I shall dress you."

She went to her trunk and produced the picture. It was not a photograph, but a little crayon head—the head of a handsome man, whose expression was a singular combination of dreaminess and alertness. It was a fascinating face.

" One of his friends did it," said Miss Ferrol. " His friends are very fond of him and admire his good looks very much. They protest against his being photographed. They like to sketch him. They are always making ' studies ' of his head. What do you think of him ? "

Louisiana hesitated.

" He is different," she said at last. " I thought he would be."

She gave the picture back to Miss Ferrol, who replaced it in her trunk. She sat for a few seconds looking down at the carpet and apparently seeing very little. Then she looked up at her companion, who was suddenly a little embarrassed at finding her receive her whimsical planning so seriously. She herself had not thought of it as being serious at all. It would be interesting and amusing, and would prove her theory.

" I will do what you want me to do," said Louisiana.

. " Then," said Miss Ferrol, wondering at an un-

2*

expected sense of discomfort in herself, " I will
dress you for supper now.　You must begin to
wear the things, so that you may get used to
them."

CHAPTER IV.

A NEW TYPE.

WHEN the two entered the supper-room to-gether a little commotion was caused by their arrival. At first the supple young figure in violet and gray was not recognized. It was not the figure people had been used to, it seemed so tall and slenderly round. The reddish-brown hair was combed high and made into soft puffs ; it made the pretty head seem more delicately shaped, and showed how white and graceful the back of the slender neck was. It was several minutes before the problem was solved. Then a sharp young woman exclaimed, *sotto voce :*

" It's the little country-girl, in new clothes—in clothes that fit. Would you believe it ? "

" Don't look at your plate so steadily," whispered Miss Ferrol. " Lean back and fan yourself as if you did not hear. You must never show that you hear things."

" I shall be obliged to give her a few hints now and then," she had said to herself beforehand. " But I feel sure when she once catches the cue she will take it."

It really seemed as if she did, too. She had looked at herself long and steadily after she had been dressed, and when she turned away from the glass she held her head a trifle more erect, and her cheeks had reddened. Perhaps what she had recognized in the reflection she had seen had taught her a lesson. But she said nothing. In a few days Olivia herself was surprised at the progress she had made. Sanguine as she was, she had not been quite prepared for the change which had taken place in her. She had felt sure it would be necessary to teach her to control her emotions, but suddenly she seemed to have learned to control them without being told to do so ; she was no longer demonstrative of her affection, she no longer asked innocent questions, nor did she ever speak of her family. Her reserve was puzzling to Olivia.

" You are very clever," she said to her one day, the words breaking from her in spite of herself, after she had sat regarding her in silence for a few minutes. " You are even cleverer than I thought you were, Louise."

" Was that very clever ? " the girl asked.

" Yes, it was," Olivia answered, " but not so clever as you are proving yourself."

But Louisiana did not smile or blush, as she had expected she would. She sat very quietly, showing neither pleasure nor shyness, and seeming for a moment or so to be absorbed in thought.

In the evening when the stages came in they were sitting on the front gallery together. As the old rattletraps bumped and swung themselves up the gravel drive, Olivia bent forward to obtain a better view of the passengers.

" He ought to be among them," she said.

Louisiana laid her hand on her arm.

" Who is that sitting with the driver ? " she asked, as the second vehicle passed them. " Isn't that——"

" To be sure it is ! " exclaimed Miss Ferrol.

She would have left her seat, but she found herself detained. Her companion had grasped her wrist.

" Wait a minute ! " she said. " Don't leave me ! Oh—I wish I had not done it ! "

Miss Ferrol turned and stared at her in amazement.

She spoke in her old, uncontrolled, childish fashion. She was pale, and her eyes were dilated.

" What is the matter?" said Miss Ferrol, hurriedly, when she found her voice. " Is it that you
really don't like the idea? If you don't, there is
no need of our carrying it out. It was only nonsense—I beg your pardon for not seeing that it
disturbed you. Perhaps, after all, it was very bad
taste in me——"

But she was not allowed to finish her sentence.
As suddenly as it had altered before, Louisiana's
expression altered again. She rose to her feet
with a strange little smile. She looked into Miss
Ferrol's astonished face steadily and calmly.

" Your brother has seen you and is coming
toward us," she said. " I will leave you. We
shall see each other again at supper."

And with a little bow she moved away with
an air of composure which left her instructress
stunned. She could scarcely recover her equilib-
rium sufficiently to greet her brother decently
when he reached her side. She had never been
so thoroughly at sea in her life.

After she had gone to her room that night, her
brother came and knocked at the door.

When she opened it and let him in he walked
to a chair and threw himself into it, wearing a
rather excited look.

"Olivia," he began at once, "what a bewildering girl!"

Olivia sat down opposite to him, with a composed smile.

"Miss Rogers, of course?" she said.

"Of course," he echoed. And then, after a pause of two or three seconds, he added, in the tone he had used before: "What a delightfully mysterious girl!"

"Mysterious!" repeated Olivia.

"There is no other word for it! She has such an adorable face, she looks so young, and she says so little." And then, with serious delight, he added: "It is a new type!"

Olivia began to laugh.

"Why are you laughing?" he demanded.

"Because I was so sure you would say that," she answered. "I was waiting for it."

"But it is true," he replied, quite vehemently. "I never saw anything like her before. I look at her great soft eyes and I catch glimpses of expression which don't seem to belong to the rest of her. When I see her eyes I could fancy for a moment that she had been brought up in a convent or had lived a very simple, isolated life, but when she speaks and moves I am bewildered. I want to hear her talk, but she says so little. She does not even dance. I suppose her relatives are serious people. I dare say you have not heard much of them from her. Her reserve is so extraordinary in a girl. I wonder how old she is?"

" Nineteen, I think."

" I thought so. I never saw anything prettier than her quiet way when I asked her to dance with me. She said, simply, ' I do not dance. I have never learned.' It was as if she had never thought of it as being an unusual thing."

He talked of her all the time he remained in the room. Olivia had never seen him so interested before.

" The fascination is that she seems to be two creatures at once," he said. " And one of them is stronger than the other and will break out and reveal itself one day. I begin by feeling I do not understand her, and that is the most interesting of all beginnings. I long to discover which of the two creatures is the real one."

When he was going away he stopped suddenly to say :

" How was it you never mentioned her in your letters? I can't understand that."

" I wanted you to see her for yourself," Olivia answered. " I thought I would wait."

" Well," he said, after thinking a moment, " I am glad, after all, that you did."

CHAPTER V.

"I HAVE HURT YOU."

FROM the day of his arrival a new life began for Louisiana. She was no longer an obscure and unconsidered young person. Suddenly, and for the first time in her life, she found herself vested with a marvellous power. It was a power girls of a different class from her own are vested with from the beginning of their lives. They are used to it and regard it as their birthright. Louisiana was not used to it. There had been nothing like it attending her position as "that purty gal o' Rogerses." She was accustomed to the admiration of men she was indifferent to—men who wore short-waisted blue-jean coats, and turned upon their elbows to stare at her as she sat in the little white frame church. After making an effort to cultivate her acquaintance, they generally went away disconcerted. "She's mighty still," they said. "She haint got nothin' to say. Seems like thar aint much to her—but she's powerful purty though."

This was nothing like her present experience. She began slowly to realize that she was a little like a young queen now. Here was a man such as she had never spoken to before, who was always ready to endeavor to his utmost to please her: who, without any tendency toward sentimental nonsense, was plainly the happier for her presence and favor. What could be more assiduous and gallant than the every-day behavior of the well-bred, thoroughly experienced young man of the period toward the young beauty who for the moment reigns over his fancy! It need only be over his fancy; there is no necessity that the impression should be any deeper. His suavity, his chivalric air, his ready wit in her service, are all that could be desired.

When Louisiana awakened to the fact that all this homage was rendered to her as being only the natural result of her girlish beauty—as if it was the simplest thing in the world, and a state of affairs which must have existed from the first—she experienced a sense of terror. Just at the very first she would have been glad to escape from it and sink into her old obscurity.

" It does not belong to me," she said to herself.

" It belongs to some one else—to the girl he thinks I am. I am not that girl, though ; I will remember that."

But in a few days she calmed down. She told herself that she always did remember, but she ceased to feel frightened and was more at ease. She never talked very much, but she became more familiar with the subjects she heard discussed. One morning she went to Olivia's room and asked her for the address of a bookseller.

" I want to send for some books and—and magazines," she said, confusedly. " I wish you—if you would tell me what to send for. Father will give me the money if I ask him for it."

Olivia sat down and made a list. It was a long list, comprising the best periodicals of the day and several standard books.

When she handed it to her she regarded her with curiosity.

" You mean to read them all ?" she asked.

" Isn't it time that I should ? " replied her pupil.

" Well—it is a good plan," returned Olivia, rather absently.

Truth to tell, she was more puzzled every day. She had begun to be quite sure that something had happened. It seemed as if a slight coldness existed between herself and her whilom adorer. The simplicity of her enthusiasm was gone. Her affection had changed as her outward bearing. It was a better regulated and less noticeable emotion. Once or twice Olivia fancied she had seen the girl looking at her even sadly, as if she felt, for the moment, a sense of some loss.

" Perhaps it was very clumsy in me," she used to say to herself. " Perhaps I don't understand her, after all."

But she could not help looking on with interest. She had never before seen Laurence enjoy himself so thoroughly. He had been working very hard during the past year, and was ready for his holiday. He found the utter idleness, which was the chief feature of the place, a good thing. There was no town or village within twenty miles, newspapers were a day or two old when they arrived, there were very few books to be found, and there was absolutely no excitement. At night the band brayed in the empty-looking ball-room, and a few very young couples danced, in a desultory fashion and without any ceremony. The primitive, domesticated slowness of the place was charming. Most of the guests had come from the far South at the beginning of the season and would remain until the close of it ; so they had had time to be-

come familiar with each other and to throw aside
restraint.

" There is nothing to distract one," Ferrol said,
" nothing to rouse one, nothing to inspire one—
nothing ! It is delicious ! Why didn't I know
of it before ? "

He had plenty of time to study his sister's
friend. She rode and walked with him and
Olivia when they made their excursions, she
listened while he read aloud to them as he lay
on the grass in a quiet corner of the grounds.
He thought her natural reserve held her from
expressing her opinion on what he read very
freely ; it certainly did not occur to him that she
was beginning her literary education under his
guidance. He could see that the things which
pleased him most were not lost upon her. Her
face told him that. One moonlight night, as
they sat on an upper gallery, he began to speak
of the novelty of the aspect of the country as it
presented itself to an outsider who saw it for the
first time.

" It is a new life, and a new people," he said.
" And, by the way, Olivia, where is the new
species of young woman I was to see—the
daughter of the people who does not belong to
her sphere ? "

He turned to Louisiana.

"Have you ever seen her?" he asked. "I must confess to a dubiousness on the subject."

Before he could add another word Louisiana turned upon him. He could see her face clearly in the moonlight. It was white, and her eyes were dilated and full of fire.

"Why do you speak in that way?" she cried. "As if—as if such people were so far beneath you. What right have you——"

She stopped suddenly. Laurence Ferrol was gazing at her in amazement. She rose from her seat, trembling.

"I will go away a little," she said. "I beg your pardon—and Miss Ferrol's."

She turned her back upon them and went away. Ferrol sat holding her little round, white-feather fan helplessly, and staring after her until she disappeared.

It was several seconds before the silence was broken. It was he who broke it.

"I don't know what it means," he said, in a low voice. "I don't know what I have done!"

In a little while he got up and began to roam aimlessly about the gallery. He strolled from one end to the other with his hands thrust in his coat pockets. Olivia, who had remained seated, knew that he was waiting in hopes that Louisiana would return. He had been walking to and fro, looking as miserable as possible, for about half an hour, when at last she saw him pause and turn half round before the open door of an upper corridor leading out upon the verandah. A black figure stood revealed against the inside light. It was Louisiana, and, after hesitating a moment, she moved slowly forward.

She had not recovered her color, but her manner was perfectly quiet.

" I am glad you did not go away," she said.

Ferrol had only stood still at first, waiting her pleasure, but the instant she spoke he made a quick step toward her.

" I should have felt it a very hard thing not to have seen you again before I slept," he said.

She made no reply, and they walked together in silence until they reached the opposite end of the gallery.

" Miss Ferrol has gone in," she said then.

He turned to look and saw that such was the case. Suddenly, for some reason best known to herself, Olivia had disappeared from the scene.

Louisiana leaned against one of the slender, supporting pillars of the gallery. She did not look at Ferrol, but at the blackness of the mountains rising before them. Ferrol could not look away from her.

"If you had not come out again," he said, after a pause, "I think I should have remained here, baying at the moon, all night."

Then, as she made no reply, he began to pour himself forth quite recklessly.

"I cannot quite understand how I hurt you," he said. "It seemed to me that I must have hurt you, but even while I don't understand, there are no words abject enough to express what I feel now and have felt during the last half hour. If I only dared ask you to tell me——"

She stopped him.

"I can't tell you," she said. "But it is not your fault—it is nothing you could have understood—it is my fault—all my fault, and—I deserve it."

He was terribly discouraged.

"I am bewildered," he said. "I am very unhappy."

She turned her pretty, pale face round to him swiftly.

"It is not you who need be unhappy," she exclaimed. "It is I!"

The next instant she had checked herself again, just as she had done before.

" Let us talk of something else," she said, coldly.

" It will not be easy for me to do so," he answered, " but I will try."

Before Olivia went to bed she had a visit from her.

She received her with some embarrassment, it must be confessed. Day by day she felt less at ease with her and more deeply self-convicted of some blundering,—which, to a young woman of her temperament, was a sharp penalty.

Louisiana would not sit down. She revealed her purpose in coming at once.

" I want to ask you to make me a promise," she said, " and I want to ask your pardon."

" Don't do that," said Olivia.

" I want you to promise that you will not tell your brother the truth until you have left here and are at home. I shall go away very soon. I am tired of what I have been doing. It is different from what you meant it to be. But you must promise that if you stay after I have gone—as of course you will—you will not tell him. My home is only a few miles away. You might be tempted, after thinking it over, to come and see me—and I should not like it. I want it all to stop here—I mean my part of it. I don't want to know the rest."

Olivia had never felt so helpless in her life. She had neither self-poise, nor tact, nor any other daring quality left.

" I wish," she faltered, gazing at the girl quite pathetically, " I wish we had never begun it."

" So do I," said Louisiana. " Do you promise ? "

" Y-yes. I would promise anything. I—I have hurt your feelings," she confessed, in an outbreak.

She was destined to receive a fresh shock. All at once the girl was metamorphosed again. It was her old ignorant, sweet, simple self who stood there, with trembling lips and dilated eyes.

" Yes, you have ! " she cried. " Yes, you have ! "

And she burst into tears and turned about and ran out of the room.

CHAPTER VI.

THE ROAD TO THE RIGHT.

THE morning after, Ferrol heard an announcement which came upon him like a clap of thunder.

After breakfast, as they walked about the grounds, Olivia, who had seemed to be in an abstracted mood, said, without any preface :

" Miss Rogers returns home to-morrow."

Laurence stopped short in the middle of the path.

" To-morrow ! " he exclaimed. " Oh, no."

He glanced across at Louisiana with an anxious face.

" Yes," she said, " I am going home."

" To New York ? "

" I do not live in New York."

She spoke quite simply, but the words were a shock to him. They embarrassed him. There was no coldness in her manner, no displeasure in her tone, but, of course, he understood that it would be worse than tactless to inquire further. Was it possible that she did not care that he should know where she lived ? There seemed no other construction to be placed upon her words. He flushed a little, and for a few minutes looked rather gloomy, though he quickly recovered himself afterward and changed the subject with creditable readiness.

" Did not you tell me she lived in New York ? " he asked Olivia, the first time they were alone together.

" No," Olivia answered, a trifle sharply. " Why New York, more than another place ? "

" For no reason whatever,—really," he returned, more bewildered than ever. " There *was* no reason why I should choose New York, only when I spoke to her of certain places there, she —she——"

He paused and thought the matter over carefully before finishing his sentence. He ended it at last in a singular manner.

" She said nothing," he said. " It is actually true —now I think of it—she said nothing whatever ! "

" And because she said nothing whatever——" began Olivia.

He drew his hand across his forehead with a puzzled gesture.

" I fancied she *looked* as if she knew," he said, slowly. " I am sure she looked as if she knew what I was talking about—as if she knew the places, I mean. It is very queer ! There seems no reason in it. Why shouldn't she wish us to know where she lives ? "

" I—I must confess," cried Olivia, " that I am getting a little tired of her."

It was treacherous and vicious, and she knew it was ; but her guilty conscience and her increasing sense of having bungled drove her to desperation. If she had not promised to keep the truth to herself, she would have been only too glad to unburden herself. It was so stupid, after all, and she had only herself to blame.

Laurence drew a long breath.

" You cannot be tired of *her !* " he said. " That is impossible. She takes firmer hold upon one every hour."

This was certainly true, as far as he was concerned. He was often even surprised at his own enthusiasm. He had seen so many pretty women that it was almost inconsistent that he should be so much moved by the prettiness of one charming creature, and particularly one who spoke so little, who, after all, was—but there he always found himself at a full stop. He could not say what she was, he did not know yet; really, he seemed no nearer the solution of the mystery than he had been at first. There lay the fascination. He felt so sure there was an immense deal for him to discover, if he could only discover it. He had an ideal in his mind, and this ideal, he felt confident, was the real creature, if he could only see her. During the episode on the upper gallery he fancied he had caught a glimpse of what was to be revealed. The sudden passion on her pale young face, the fire in her eyes, were what he had dreamed of.

If he had not been possessed of courage and an honest faith in himself, born of a goodly amount of success, he would have been far more depressed than he was. She was going away, and had not encouraged him to look forward to their meeting again.

" I own it is rather bad to look at," he said to himself, " if one quite believed that Fate would serve one such an ill turn. She never played me such a trick, however, and I won't believe she will. I shall see her again—sometime. It will turn out fairly enough, surely."

So with this consolation he supported himself. There was one day left and he meant to make the best of it. It was to be spent in driving to a certain mountain, about ten miles distant. All tourists who were possessed of sufficient energy made this excursion as a matter of duty, if from no more enthusiastic motive. A strong, light carriage and a pair of horses were kept in the hotel stables for the express purpose of conveying guests to this special point.

This vehicle Ferrol had engaged the day before, and as matters had developed he had cause to congratulate himself upon the fact. He said to Louisiana what he had before said to himself:

"We have one day left, and we will make the best of it."

Olivia, who stood upon the gallery before which the carriage had been drawn up, glanced at Louisiana furtively. On her part she felt privately that it would be rather hard to make the best of it. She wished that it was well over. But Louisiana did not return her glance. She was looking at Ferrol and the horses. She had done something new this morning. She had laid aside her borrowed splendor and attired herself in one of her own dresses, which she had had the boldness to remodel. She had seized a hint from some one of Olivia's possessions, and had given her costume a pretty air of primitive simplicity. It was a plain white lawn, with a little frilled cape or fichu which crossed upon her breast, and was knotted loosely behind. She had a black velvet ribbon around her lithe waist, a rose in her bosom where the fichu crossed, and a broad Gainsborough hat upon her head. One was reminded somewhat of the picturesque young woman of the good old colony times. Ferrol, at least, when he first caught sight of her, was reminded of pictures he had seen of them.

There was no trace of her last night's fire in her manner. She was quieter than usual through the first part of the drive. She was gentle to submissiveness to Olivia. There was something even tender in her voice once or twice when she addressed her. Laurence noticed it, and accounted for it naturally enough.

"She is really fonder of her than she has seemed," he thought, "and she is sorry that their parting is so near."

He was just arriving at this conclusion when Louisiana touched his arm.

"Don't take that road," she said.

He drew up his horses and looked at her with surprise. There were two roads before them, and he had been upon the point of taking the one to the right.

"But it is the only road to take," he continued.

" The other does not lead to the mountain. I was told to be sure to take the road to the right hand."

" It is a mistake," she said, in a disturbed tone. " The left-hand road leads to the mountain, too— at least, we can reach it by striking the wagon-road through the woods. I—yes, I am sure of it."

" But this is the better road. Is there any reason why you prefer the other? Could you pilot us? If you can——"

He stopped and looked at her appealingly.

He was ready to do anything she wished, but the necessity for his yielding had passed. Her face assumed a set look.

" I can't," she answered. " Take the road to the right. Why not?"

3*

CHAPTER VII.

" SHE AINT YERE."

FERROL was obliged to admit when they turned
their faces homeward that the day was hardly a
success, after all. Olivia had not been at her best,
for some reason or other, and from the moment
they had taken the right-hand road Louisiana had
been wholly incomprehensible.

In her quietest mood she had never worn a cold
air before ; to-day she had been cold and unre-
sponsive. It had struck him that she was absorbed in thinking of something which was quite
beyond him. She was plainly not thinking of
him, nor of Olivia, nor of the journey they were
making. During the drive she had sat with her
hands folded upon her lap, her eyes fixed straight
before her. She had paid no attention to the
scenery, only rousing herself to call their attention to one object. This object was a house they
passed—the rambling, low-roofed white house of

some well-to-do farmer. It was set upon a small hill and had a long front porch, mottled with blue and white paint in a sanguine attempt at imitating variegated marble.

She burst into a low laugh when she saw it.

"Look at that," she said. "That is one of the finest houses in the country. The man who owns it is counted a rich man among his neighbors."

Ferrol put up his eye-glasses to examine it. (It is to be deplored that he was a trifle near-sighted.)

"By George!" he said. "That is an idea, isn't it, that marble business! I wonder who did it? Do you know the man who lives there?"

"I have heard of him," she answered, "from several people. He is a namesake of mine. His name is Rogers."

When they returned to their carriage, after a ramble up the mountain-side, they became conscious that the sky had suddenly darkened. Ferrol looked up, and his face assumed a rather serious expression.

"If either of you is weather-wise," he said, "I wish you would tell me what that cloud means. You have been among the mountains longer than I have."

Louisiana glanced upward quickly.

"It means a storm," she said, "and a heavy one. We shall be drenched in half an hour."

Ferrol looked at her white dress and the little frilled fichu, which was her sole protection.

"Oh, but that won't do!" he exclaimed. "What insanity in me not to think of umbrellas!"

"Umbrellas!" echoed Louisiana. "If we had each six umbrellas they could not save us. We may as well get into the carriage. We are only losing time."

They were just getting in when an idea struck Ferrol which caused him to utter an exclamation of ecstatic relief.

"Why," he cried, "there is that house we passed! Get in quickly. We can reach there in twenty minutes."

Louisiana had her foot upon the step. She stopped short and turned to face him. She changed from red to white and from white to red again, as if with actual terror.

"There!" she exclaimed. "There!"

"Yes," he answered. "We can reach there in time to save ourselves. Is there any objection to our going,—in the last extremity?"

For a second they looked into each other's

eyes, **and** then she turned and sprang into the carriage. She laughed aloud.

" Oh, no," she said. " Go there ! It will be a nice place to **stay—and** the people will amuse you. Go there."

They reached the house in a quarter of an hour instead of twenty minutes. They had driven fast and kept ahead of the storm, but when they drew up before the picket fence the clouds were black and the thunder was rolling behind them.

It was Louisiana who got out first. She led the way up the path to the house and mounted the steps of the variegated porch. She did not knock at the door, which stood **open, but,** somewhat to Ferrol's amazement, walked at once into the front room, which was plainly the room of state. Not to put too fine a point upon it, it was a hideous room.

The ceiling was **so** low that Ferrol **felt** as if he must knock his head against it ; it was papered — ceiling and all — with paper **of** an unwholesome yellow enlivened with large blue flowers ; there was a bedstead in one **corner,** and the walls were ornamented with colored lithographs of moon-faced houris, with round **eyes** and round, red cheeks, and wearing low-necked dresses, **and** flowers in their bosoms, and bright yellow gold necklaces. These works of art were the first things which caught Ferrol's eye, and he went slowly up to the most remarkable, and stood before it, regarding it with mingled wonderment and awe.

He turned from it after a few seconds to look at Louisiana, who stood near him, and he beheld what seemed to him a phenomenon. He had never seen her blush before as other women blush —now she was blushing, burning red from chin to brow.

" There—there is no one in this part of the house," she said. " I—I know more of these people than you do. I will go and try to find some one."

She was gone before he could interpose. Not that he would have interposed, perhaps. Somehow—without knowing why—he felt as if she did know more of the situation than he did—almost as if she were, in a manner, doing the honors for the time being.

She crossed the passage with a quick, uneven step, and made her way, as if well used to the place, into the kitchen at the back of the house.

A stout negro woman stood at a table, filling a pan with newly made biscuits. Her back was toward the door and she did not see who entered.

"Aunt Cassandry," the girl began, when the woman turned toward her.

"Who's dar?" she exclaimed. "Lor', honey, how ye skeert me! I aint no C'sandry."

The face she turned was a strange one, and it showed no sign of recognition of her visitor.

It was an odd thing that the sight of her unfamiliar face should have been a shock to Louisiana; but it was a shock. She put her hand to her side.

"Where is my—where is Mr. Rogers?" she asked. "I want to see him."

"Out on de back po'ch, honey, right now. Dar he goes!"

The girl heard him, and flew out to meet him. Her heart was throbbing hard, and she was drawing quick, short breaths.

"Father!" she cried. "Father! Don't go in the house!"

And she caught him by both shoulders and drew him round. He did not know her at first in her fanciful-simple dress and her Gainsborough hat. He was not used to that style of thing, believing that it belonged rather to the world of pictures. He stared at her. Then he broke out with an exclamation,

"Lo-rd! Louisianny!"

She kept her eyes on his face. They were feverishly bright, and her cheeks were hot. She laughed hysterically.

"Don't speak loud," she said. "There are some strange people in the house, and—and I want to tell you something."

He was a slow man, and it took him some time to grasp the fact that she was really before him in the flesh. He said, again:

"Lord, Louisianny!" adding, cheerfully, "How ye've serprised me!"

Then he took in afresh the change in her dress. There was a pile of stove-wood stacked on the porch to be ready for use, and he sat down on it to look at her.

"Why, ye've got a new dress on!" he said. "Thet thar's what made ye look sorter curis. I hardly knowed ye."

Then he remembered what she had said on first seeing him.

"Why don't ye want me to go in the house?" he asked. "What sort o' folks air they?"

"They came with me from the Springs," she answered; "and—and I want to—to play a joke on them."

She put her hands up to her burning cheeks, and stood so.

" A joke on 'em ? " he repeated.

" Yes," she said, speaking very fast. " They don't know I live here, they think I came from some city,—they took the notion themselves,—and I want to let them think so until we go away from the house. It will be such a good joke."

She tried to laugh, but broke off in the middle of a harsh sound. Her father, with one copperas-colored leg crossed over the other, was chewing his tobacco slowly, after the manner of a ruminating animal, while he watched her.

" Don't you see ? " she asked.

" Wa-al, no," he answered. " Not rightly."

She actually assumed a kind of spectral gayety.

" I never thought of it until I saw it was not Cassandry who was in the kitchen," she said. " The woman who is there didn't know me, and it came into my mind that—that we might play off on them," using the phraseology to which he was the most accustomed.

" Waal, we mought," he admitted, with a speculative deliberateness. " Thet's so. We mought —if thar was any use in it."

" It's only for a joke," she persisted, hurriedly.

" Thet's so," he repeated. " Thet's so."

He got up slowly and rather lumberingly from

his seat and dusted the chips from his copperas-
colored legs.

" Hev ye ben enjyin' yerself, Louisianny ? " he
asked.

" Yes," she answered. " Never better."

" Ye must hev," he returned, " or ye wouldn't
be in sperrits to play jokes."

Then he changed his tone so suddenly that she
was startled.

" What do ye want me to do? " he asked.

She put her hand on his shoulder and tried to
laugh again.

" To pretend you don't know me—to pretend
I have never been here before. That's joke
enough, isn't it? They will think so when I tell
them the truth. You slow old father! Why
don't you laugh ? "

" P'r'aps," he said, " it's on account o' me bein'
slow, Louisianny. Mebbe I shall begin arter a
while."

" Don't begin at the wrong time," she said,
still keeping up her feverish laugh, " or you'll
spoil it all. Now come along in and—and pretend you don't know me," she continued, drawing him forward by the arm. " They might sus-
pect something if we stay so long. All you've
got to do is to pretend you don't know me."

"Thet's so, Louisianny," with a kindly glance downward at her excited face as he followed her out. "Thar aint no call fur me to do nothin' else, is there—just pretend I don't know ye?"

It was wonderful how well he did it, too. When she preceded him into the room the girl was quivering with excitement. He might break down, and it would be all over in a second. But she looked Ferrol boldly in the face when she made her first speech.

"This is the gentleman of the house," she said. "I found him on the back porch. He had just come in. He has been kind enough to say we may stay until the storm is over."

"Oh, yes," said he hospitably, "stay an' welcome. Ye aint the first as has stopped over. Storms come up sorter suddent, an' we haint the kind as turns folks away."

Ferrol thanked him, Olivia joining in with a murmur of gratitude. They were very much indebted to him for his hospitality; they considered themselves very fortunate.

Their host received their protestations with much equanimity.

"If ye'd like to set out on the front porch and watch the storm come up," he said, "thar's seats thar. Or would ye druther set here? Women-folks is gen'rally fond o' settin' in-doors whar thar's a parlor."

But they preferred the porch, and followed him out upon it.

Having seen them seated, he took a chair himself. It was a split-seated chair, painted green, and he tilted it back against a pillar of the porch and applied himself to the full enjoyment of a position more remarkable for ease than elegance. Ferrol regarded him with stealthy rapture, and drank in every word he uttered.

" This," he had exclaimed delightedly to Olivia, in private—" why, this is delightful! These are the people we have read of. I scarcely believed in them before. I would not have missed it for the world ! "

" In gin'ral, now," their entertainer proceeded, " wimmin-folk is fonder o' settin' in parlors. My wife was powerful sot on her parlor. She wasn't never satisfied till she hed one an' hed it fixed up to her notion. She was allers tradin' fur picters fur it. She tuk a heap o' pride in her picters. She allers had it in her mind that her little gal should have a showy parlor when she growed up."

" You have a daughter ? " said Ferrol.

Their host hitched his chair a little to one side.

He bent forward to expectorate, and then answered with his eyes fixed upon some distant point toward the mountains.

"Wa–al, yes," he said; "but she aint yere, Louisianny aint."

Miss Ferrol gave a little start, and immediately made an effort to appear entirely at ease.

"Did you say," asked Ferrol, "that your daughter's name was ——"

"Louisianny," promptly. "I come from thar."

Louisiana got up and walked to the opposite end of the porch.

"The storm will be upon us in a few minutes," she said. "It is beginning to rain now. Come and look at this cloud driving over the mountain-top."

Ferrol rose and went to her. He stood for a moment looking at the cloud, but plainly not thinking of it.

"His daughter's name is Louisiana," he said, in an undertone. "Louisiana! Isn't that delicious?"

Suddenly, even as he spoke, a new idea occurred to him.

"Why," he exclaimed, "your name is Louise, isn't it? I think Olivia said so."

"Yes," she answered, "my name is Louise."

"How should you have liked it," he inquired, absent-mindedly, "if it had been Louisiana?"

She answered him with a hard coolness which it startled him afterward to remember.

' How would you have liked it?" she said.

They were driven back just then by the rain, which began to beat in upon their end of the porch. They were obliged to return to Olivia and Mr. Rogers, who were engaged in an animated conversation.

The fact was that, in her momentary excitement, Olivia had plunged into conversation as a refuge. She had suddenly poured forth a stream of remark and query which had the effect of spurring up her companion to a like exhibition of frankness. He had been asking questions, too.

"She's ben tellin' me," he said, as Ferrol approached, "thet you're a littery man, an' write fur the papers—novel-stories, an' pomes an' things. I never seen one before—not as I know on."

"I wonder why not!" remarked Ferrol. "We are plentiful enough."

"Air ye now?" he asked reflectively. "I had an idee thar was only one on ye now an' ag'in— jest now an' ag'in."

He paused there to shake his head.

"I've often wondered how ye could do it," he said. "*I* couldn't. Thar's some as thinks they could if they tried, but I wa'n't never thataway— I wa'n't never thataway. I haint no idee I could do it, not if I tried ever so. Seems to me," he went on, with the air of making an announcement of so novel a nature that he must present it modestly, "seems to me, now, as if them as does it must hev a kinder gift fur it, now. Lord! I couldn't write a novel. I wouldn't know whar to begin."

"It is difficult to decide where," said Ferrol.

He did not smile at all. His manner was perfect—so full of interest, indeed, that Mr. Rogers quite warmed and expanded under it.

"The scenes on 'em all, now, bein' mostly laid in Bagdad, would be agin me, if nothin' else war," he proceeded.

"Being laid—— ?" queried Ferrol.

"In Bagdad or—wa-al, furrin parts tharabouts. Ye see I couldn't tell nothin' much about no place but North Ca'liny, an' folks wouldn't buy it."

"But why not?" exclaimed Ferrol.

"Why, Lord bless ye!" he said, hilariously, "they'd know it wa'n't true. They'd say in a minnit: 'Why, thar's thet fool Rogers ben a writin' a pack o' lies thet aint a word on it true.

Thar aint no cas-tles in Hamilton County, an' thar aint no folks like these yere. It just aint so!' I 'lowed thet thar was the reason the novel-writers allers writ about things a-happenin' in Bagdad. Ye kin say most anythin' ye like about Bagdad an' no one cayn't contradict ye."

" I don't seem to remember many novels of—of that particular description," remarked Ferrol, in a rather low voice. " Perhaps my memory——"

" Ye don't?" he queried, in much surprise. "Waal now, jest you notice an' see if it aint so. I haint read many novels myself. I haint read but one——"

" Oh!" interposed Ferrol. " And it was a story of life in Bagdad."

" Yes; an' I've heard tell of others as was the same. Hance Claiborn, now, he was a-tellen me of one."

He checked himself to speak to the negro woman who had presented herself at a room door.

" We're a-comin', Nancy," he said, with an air of good-fellowship. " Now, ladies an' gentlemen," he added, rising from his chair, " walk in an' have some supper."

Ferrol and Olivia rose with some hesitation.

" You are very kind," they said. " We did not intend to give you trouble."

"Trouble!" he replied, as if scarcely comprehending. "This yere aint no trouble. Ye haint ben in North Ca'liny before, hev ye?" he continued, good-naturedly. "We're bound to hev ye eat, if ye stay with us long enough. We wouldn't let ye go 'way without eatin', bless ye. We aint that kind. Walk straight in."

He led them into a long, low room, half kitchen, half dining-room. It was not so ugly as the room of state, because it was entirely unadorned. Its ceiled walls were painted brown and stained with many a winter's smoke. The pine table was spread with a clean homespun cloth and heaped with well-cooked, appetizing food.

"If ye can put up with country fare, ye'll not find it so bad," said the host. "Nancy prides herself on her way o' doin' things."

There never was more kindly hospitality, Ferrol thought. The simple generosity which made them favored guests at once warmed and touched him. He glanced across at Louisiana to see if she was not as much pleased as he was himself. But the food upon her plate remained almost untouched. There was a strange look on her face; she was deadly pale and her downcast eyes shone under their lashes. She did not look at their host

4

at all ; it struck Ferrol that she avoided looking
at him with a strong effort.   Her pallor made him
anxious.

" You are not well," he said to her.   " You do
not look well at all."

Their host started and turned toward her.

" Why, no ye aint ! " he exclaimed, quite tremulously.   " Lord, no !   Ye cayn't be.   Ye haint
no color.   What—what's the trouble, Lou—Lord !
I was gwine to call ye Louisianny, an'—she aint
yere, Louisianny aint."

He ended with a nervous laugh.

" I'm used to takin' a heap o' care on her," he
said.   " I've lost ten on 'em, an' she's all that's left
me, an'—an' I think a heap on her.   I—I wish
she was yere.   Ye musn't git sick, ma'am."

The girl got up hurriedly.

" I am not sick, really," she said.   " The thunder—I have a little headache.   I will go out on
to the porch.   It's clearing up now.   The fresh
air will do me good."

The old man rose, too, with rather a flurried
manner.

" If Louisianny was yere," he faltered, "she
could give ye something to help ye.   Camphire
now—sperrits of camphire—let me git ye some."

" No—no," said the girl.   " No, thank you."

And she slipped out of the door and was gone.

Mr. Rogers sat down again with a sigh.

" I wish she'd let me git her some," he said, wistfully. " I know how it is with young critters like that. They're dele-cate," anxiously. " Lord, they're dele-cate. They'd oughter hev' their mothers round 'em. I know how it is with Louisianny."

A cloud seemed to settle upon him. He rubbed his grizzled chin with his hand again and again, glancing at the open door as he did it. It was evident that his heart was outside with the girl who was like " Louisianny."

CHAPTER VIII.

"NOTHING HAS HURT YOU.'

THE storm was quite over, and the sun was setting in flames of gold when the meal was ended and they went out on the porch again. Mr. Rogers had scarcely recovered himself, but he had made an effort to do so, and had so far succeeded as to begin to describe the nature of the one novel he had read. Still, he had rubbed his chin and kept his eye uneasily on the door all the time he had been talking.

"It was about a Frenchman," he said, seriously, "an' his name was—Frankoyse—F-r-a-n-c-o-i-s, Frankoyse. Thet thar's a French name, aint it? Me an' Ianthy 'lowed it was common to the country. It don't belong yere, Frankoyse don't, an' it's got a furrin sound."

"It—yes, it is a French name," assented Ferrol.

A few minutes afterward they went out. Louisiana stood at the end of the porch, leaning against a wooden pillar and twisting an arm around it.

"Are ye better?" Mr. Rogers asked. "I am goin' to 'tend to my stock, an' if ye aint, mebbe the camphire—sperrits of camphire——"

"I don't need it," she answered. "I am quite well."

So he went away and left them, promising to return shortly and "gear up their critters" for them that they might go on their way.

When he was gone, there was a silence of a few seconds which Ferrol could not exactly account for. Almost for the first time in his manhood, he did not know what to say. Gradually there had settled upon him the conviction that something had gone very wrong indeed, that there was something mysterious and complicated at work, that somehow he himself was involved, and that his position was at once a most singular and delicate one. It was several moments before he could decide that his best plan seemed to be to try to conceal his bewilderment and appear at ease. And, very naturally, the speech he chose to begin with was the most unlucky he could have hit upon.

"He is charming," he said. "What a lovable old fellow! What a delicious old fellow! He

has been telling me about the novel. It is the
the story of a Frenchman, and his name—try to
guess his name."

But Louisiana did not try.

"You couldn't guess it," he went on. "It is
better than all the rest. His name was—
Frankoyse."

That instant she turned round. She was shaking all over like a leaf.

"Good heavens!" flashed through his mind.
"This is a climax! *This* is the real creature!"

"Don't laugh again!" she cried. "Don't
dare to laugh! I wont bear it! He is my
father!"

For a second or so he had not the breath to
speak.

"*Your* father!" he said, when he found his
voice. "*Your* father! *Yours!*"

"Yes," she answered, "mine. This is my
home. I have lived here all my life—my name is
Louisiana. You have laughed at me too!"

It was the real creature, indeed, whom he saw.
She burst into passionate tears.

"Do you think that I kept up this pretense
to-day because I was ashamed of him?" she said.
"Do you think I did it because I did not love
him—and respect him—and think him better than

all the rest of the world? It was because I loved him so much **that** I did it—because I knew so **well** that you would say to each other that he was not like me—that he was rougher, and **that it** was **a** wonder I **belonged to him.** It is **a wonder** I **be**long to him! **I am not** worthy to kiss **his** shoes. I have been ashamed—I have been bad enough **for that, but not bad** enough to **be** ashamed of him. I thought at first it would be better to let **you** believe what you would—that it would soon be over, and we should never see each other again, **but** I did not think that I should have **to** sit by and see you laugh because he does not know the world as you do—because he has always **lived** his simple, **good life in one** simple, country place."

Ferrol had grown as pale as she was herself. He groaned aloud.

"Oh!" he cried, "**what shall I** say **to you?** For heaven's sake try to understand that it is not at him I have laughed, but——"

"He has never been away from home," she broke in. "He has worked too hard to have time to read, and—" she stopped and dropped her hands with **a** gesture of unutterable pride. "Why should **I tell you** that?" she said. "**It** sounds as if **I** were apologizing for him, and there **is no need** that I should."

"If I could understand," began Ferrol,—"if I could realize ——"

"Ask your sister," she replied. "It was her plan. I—I" (with a little sob) "am only her experiment."

Olivia came forward, looking wholly subdued. Her eyes were wet, too.

"It is true," she said. "It is all my fault."

"May I ask you to explain?" said Ferrol, rather sternly. "I suppose some of this has been for my benefit."

"Don't speak in that tone," said Olivia. "It is bad enough as it is. I—I never was so wretched in my life. I never dreamed of its turning out in this way. She was so pretty and gentle and quick to take a hint, and—I wanted to try the experiment—to see if you would guess at the truth. I—I had a theory, and I was so much interested that—I forgot to—to think of her very much. I did not think she would care."

Louisiana broke in.

"Yes," she said, her eyes bright with pain, "she forgot. I was very fond of her, and I knew so very little that she forgot to think of me. I was only a kind of plaything—but I was too proud to remind her. I thought it would be soon over, and I knew how ignorant I was. I was

afraid to trust my feelings at first. I thought perhaps—it was vanity, and I ought to crush it down.
I was very fond of her."

"Oh!" cried Olivia, piteously, "don't say
'was,' Louise!"

"Don't say 'Louise,'" was the reply. "Say
'Louisiana.' I am not ashamed of it now. I
want Mr. Ferrol to hear it."

"I have nothing to say in self-defense,"
Laurence replied, hopelessly.

"There is nothing for any of us to say but
good-by," said Louisiana. "We shall never see
each other again. It is all over between us.
You will go your way and I shall go mine. I
shall stay here to-night. You must drive back to
the Springs without me. I ought never to have
gone there."

Laurence threw himself into a chair and sat
shading his face with his hand. He stared from
under it at the shining wet grass and leaves.
Even yet he scarcely believed that all this was
true. He felt as if he were walking in a dream.
The worst of it was this desperate feeling that
there was nothing for him to say. There was a
long silence, but at last Louisiana left her place
and came and stood before him.

"I am going to meet my father," she said.

4*

" I persuaded him that I was only playing a joke. He thought it was one of my fancies, and he helped me out because I asked him to do it. I am going to tell him that I have told you the truth. He wont know why I did it. I will make it easy for you. I shall not see you again. Good-by."

Ferrol's misery got the better of him.

" I can't bear this ! " he cried, springing up. " I can't, indeed."

She drew back.

" Why not ? " she said. " Nothing has hurt *you.*"

The simple coldness of her manner was very hard upon him, indeed.

" You think I have no right to complain," he answered, " and yet see how you send me away ! You speak as if you did not intend to let me see you again——"

" No," she interposed, " you shall not see me again. Why should you ? Ask your sister to tell you how ignorant I am. She knows. Why should you come here ? There would always be as much to laugh at as there has been to-day. Go where you need not laugh. This is not the place for you. Good-by ! "

Then he knew he need say no more. She

spoke with a child's passion and with a woman's proud obstinacy. Then she turned to Olivia. He was thrilled to the heart as he watched her while she did it. Her eyes were full of tears, but she had put both her hands behind her.

" Good-by," she said.

Olivia broke down altogether.

" Is that the way you are going to say good-by ?" she cried. " I did not think you were so hard. If I had meant any harm—but I didn't— and you look as if you never would forgive me."

" I may some time," answered the girl. " I don't yet. I did not think I was so hard, either."

Her hands fell at her sides and she stood trembling a second. All at once she had broken down, too.

" I loved you," she said ; " but you did not love me."

And then she turned away and walked slowly into the house.

It was almost half an hour before their host came to them with the news that their carriage was ready.

He looked rather " off color " himself and wore a wearied air, but he was very uncommunicative.

" Louisianny 'lowed she'd go to bed an' sleep

off her headache, instead of goin' back to the Springs," he said. " I'll be thar in a day or two to 'tend to her bill an' the rest on it. I 'low the waters haint done her much good. She aint at herself rightly. I knowed she wasn't when she was so notionate this evenin'. She aint notionate when she's at herself."

" We are much indebted to you for your kindness," said Ferrol, when he took the reins.

" Oh, thet aint nothin'. You're welcome. You'd hev hed a better time if Louisianny had been at herself. Good-by to ye. Ye'll hev plenty of moonlight to see ye home."

Their long ride was a silent one When they reached the end of it and Olivia had been helped out of the carriage and stood in the moonlight upon the deserted gallery, where she had stood with Louisiana in the morning, she looked very suitably miserable.

" Laurence," she said, " I don't exactly see why you should feel so very severe about it. I am sure I am as abject as any one could wish."

He stood a moment in silence looking absently out on the moonlight-flooded lawn. Everything was still and wore an air of desolation.

" We won't talk about it," he said, at last, " but you have done me an ill-turn, Olivia."

CHAPTER IX.

"DON'T YE, LOUISIANNY?"

As HE said it, Louisiana was at home in the house-room, sitting on a low chair at her father's knee and looking into the fire. She had not gone to bed. When he returned to the house her father had found her sitting here, and she had not left her place since. A wood fire had been lighted because the mountain air was cool after the rains, and she seemed to like to sit and watch it and think.

Mr. Rogers himself was in a thoughtful mood. After leaving his departing guests he had settled down with some deliberation. He had closed the doors and brought forward his favorite wooden-backed, split-seated chair. Then he had seated himself, and drawing forth his twist of tobacco had cut off a goodly "chaw." He moved slowly and wore a serious and somewhat abstracted air. Afterward he tilted backward a little, crossed his legs, and proceeded to ruminate.

" Louisianny," he said, " Louisianny, I'd like to hear the rights of it."

She answered him in a low voice.

" It is not worth telling," she said. " It was a very poor joke, after all."

He gave her a quick side glance, rubbing his crossed legs slowly.

" Was it ? " he remarked. " A poor one, after all ? Why, thet's bad."

The quiet patience of his face was a study. He went on rubbing his leg even more slowly than before.

" Thet's bad," he said again. " Now, what d'ye think was the trouble, Louisianny ? "

" I made a mistake," she answered. " That was all."

Suddenly she turned to him and laid her folded arms on his knee and her face upon them, sobbing.

" I oughtn't to have gone," she cried. " I ought to have stayed at home with you, father."

His face flushed, and he was obliged to relieve his feelings by expectorating into the fire.

" Louisianny," he said, " I'd like to ask ye one question. Was thar anybody thar as didn't— well, as didn't show ye respect—as was slighty or free or—or onconsiderate ? Fur instants, any littery man—jest for instants, now ? "

"No, no!" she answered. "They were very kind to me always."

"Don't be afeared to tell me, Louisianny," he put it to her. "I only said 'fur instants,' havin' heern as littery men was sometimes—now an' again—thataway—now an' ag'in."

"They were very good to me," she repeated, "always."

"If they was," he returned, "I'm glad of it. I'm a-gittin' old, Louisianny, an' I haint much health—dispepsy's what tells on a man," he went on deliberately. "But if thar'd a bin any one as hed done it, I'd hev hed to settle it with him— I'd hev hed to hev settled it with him—liver or no liver."

He put his hand on her head and gave it a slow little rub, the wrong way, but tenderly.

"I aint goin' to ask ye no more questions," he said, "exceptin' one. Is thar anything ye'd like to hev done in the house—in the parlor, for instants, now—s'posin' we was to say in the parlor."

"No, no," she cried. "Let it stay as it is! Let it all stay as it is!"

"Wa-al," he said, meditatively, "ye know thar aint no reason why it should, Louisianny, if ye'd like to hev it fixed up more or different. If ye'd like a new paper—say a floweryer one—or a new

set of cheers an' things.   Up to Lawyer Hoskin's
I seen 'em with red seats to 'em, an' seemed like
they did set things off sorter.   If ye'd like to hev
some, thar aint no reason why ye shouldn't.
Things has gone purty well with me, an'—an' thar
aint none left but you, honey.   Lord!" he added,
in a queer burst of tenderness.   "Why shouldn't
ye hev things if ye want 'em?"

"I don't want them," she protested.   "I want
nothing but you."

For a moment there was a dead silence.   He
kept his eyes fixed on the fire.   He seemed to be
turning something over in his mind.   But at last
he spoke:

"Don't ye, Louisianny?" he said.

"No," she answered.   "Nothing."

And she drew his hand under her cheek and
kissed it.

He took it very quietly.

"Ye've got a kind heart, Louisianny," he said.
"Young folks gin'rally has, I think.   It's sorter
nat'ral, but Lord! thar's other things besides us
old folks, an' it's nat'ral as ye'd want 'em.   Thar's
things as kin be altered, an' thar's things as cayn't.
Let's alter them as kin.   If ye'd like a cupoly put
on the house, or, say a coat of yaller-buff paint—
Sawyer's new house is yaller buff, an' it's mighty

showy ; or a organ or a pianny, or more dressin',
ye shall have 'em. Them's things as it aint too
late to set right, an' ye shall hev 'em."

But she only cried the more in a soft, hushed
way.

"Oh, don't be so good to me," she said.
" Don't be so good and kind."

He went on as quietly as before.

" If—fur instants—it was me as was to be
altered, Louisianny, I'm afeared—I'm afeared we
couldn't do it. I'm afeared as I've been let run
too long—jest to put it that way. We mought
hev done it if we'd hev begun airlier—say forty or
fifty year back—but I'm afeared we couldn't do it
now. Not as I wouldn't be willin'—I wouldn't
hev a thing agin it, an' I'd try my best—but it's
late. Thar's whar it is. If it was me as hed to
be altered—made more moderner, an' to know
more, an' to hev more style—I'm afeared thar'd
be a heap o' trouble. Style didn't never seem to
come nat'ral to me, somehow. I'm one o' them
things as cayn't be altered., Let's alter them as
kin."

"I don't want you altered," she protested.
" Oh ! why should I, when you are such a good
father—such a dear father ! "

And there was a little silence again, and at the

end of it he said, in a gentle, forbearing voice, just as he had said before :

" Don't ye, Louisianny ? "

They sat silent again for some time afterward—indeed, but little more was said until they separated for the night. Then, when she kissed him and clung for a moment round his neck, he suddenly roused himself from his prolonged reverie.

" Lord !" he said, quite cheerfully, "it caynt last long, at the longest, arter all—an' you're young yet, you're young."

" What can't last long ? " she asked, timidly.

He looked into her eyes and smiled.

" Nothin'," he answered, " nothin' caynt. Nothin' don't—an' you're young."

And he was so far moved by his secret thought that he smoothed her hair from her forehead the wrong way again with a light touch, before he let her go.

CHAPTER X.

THE GREAT WORLD.

THE next morning he went to the Springs.

" I'll go an' settle up and bring ye your trunk an' things," he said. " Mebbe I mayn't git back till to-morrer, so don't ye be oneasy. Ef I feel tired when I git thar, I'll stay overnight."

She did not think it likely he would stay. She had never known him to remain away from home during a night unless he had been compelled to do so by business. He had always been too childishly fond of his home to be happy away from it. He liked the routine he had been used to through forty years, the rising at daylight, the regular common duties he assumed as his share, his own seat on the hearth or porch and at table.

" Folks may be clever enough," he used to say. "They air clever, as a rule—but it don't come nat'ral to be away. Thar aint nothin' like home an' home ways."

But he did not return that night, or even the next morning. It was dusk the next evening before Louisiana heard the buggy wheels on the road.

She had been sitting on the porch and rose to greet him when he drove up and descended from his conveyence rather stiffly.

" Ye wasn't oneasy, was ye ? " he asked.

" No," she answered ; " only it seemed strange to know you were away."

" I haint done it but three times since me an' Ianthy was married," he said. " Two o' them times was Conference to Barnsville, an' one was when Marcelly died."

When he mounted the porch steps he looked up at her with a smile on his weather-beaten face.

" Was ye lonesome ? " he asked. " I bet ye was."

" A little," she replied. " Not very."

She gave him his chair against the wooden pillar, and watched him as he tilted back and balanced himself on its back legs. She saw something new and disturbed in his face and manner. It was as if the bit of outside life he had seen had left temporary traces upon him. She wondered very much how it had impressed him and what he was thinking about.

And after a short time he told her.

" Ye must be lonesome," he said, " arter stay-
in' down thar. It's nat'ral. A body don't know
until they see it theirselves. It's gay thar. Lord,
yes ! it's gay, an' what suits young folks is to be
gay."

" Some of the people who were there did not
think it was gay," Louisiana said, a little listlessly.
'' They were used to gayer places and they often
called it dull, but it seemed very gay to me."

" I shouldn't want it no gayer, myself," he returned, seriously. "Not if I was young folks.
Thar must hev bin three hundred on 'em in thet
thar dinin'-room. The names o' the vittles writ
down on paper to pick an' choose from, an' fifty
or sixty waiters flyin' round. An' the dressin'!
I sot an' watched 'em as they come in. I sot an'
watched 'em all day. Thar was a heap o' cur'osi-
ties in the way of dressin' I never seen before. I
I went into the dancin'-room at night, too, an' sot
thar a spell an' watched 'em. They played a
play. Some on 'em put little caps an' aperns on,
an' rosettes an' fixin's. They sorter danced in it,
an' they hed music while they was doin' it. It
was purty, too, if a body could hev follered it
out."

" It is a dance they call the German," said Louisiana, remembering with a pang the first night she had seen it, as she sat at her new friend's side.

" German, is it ? " he said, with evident satisfaction at making the discovery. " Waal now, I ain't surprised. It hed a kinder Dutch look to me—kinder Dutch an' furrin."

Just then Nancy announced that his supper was ready, and he went in, but on the threshold he stopped and spoke again :

" Them folks as was here," he said, " they'd gone. They started the next mornin' arter they was here. They live up North somewhars, an' they've went thar."

After he had gone in, Louisiana sat still for a little while. The moon was rising and she watched it until it climbed above the tree-tops and shone bright and clear. Then one desperate little sob broke from her—only one, for she choked the next in its birth, and got up and turned toward the house and the room in which the kerosene lamp burned on the supper table.

" I'll go an' talk to him," she said. " He likes to have me with him, and it will be better than sitting here."

She went in and sat near him, resting her elbows

upon the table and her chin on her hands, and tried to begin to talk. But it was not very easy. She found that she had a tendency to fall back in long silent pauses, in which she simply looked at him with sad, tender eyes.

"I stopped at Casey's as I came on," he said, at last. "Thet thar was one thing as made me late. Thar's—thar's somethin' I hed on my mind fur him to do fur me."

"For Casey to do?" she said.

He poured his coffee into his saucer and answered with a heavy effort at speaking unconcernedly.

"I'm agoin' to hev him fix the house," he said.

She was going to ask him what he meant to have done, but he did not give her time.

"Ianthy an' me," he said, "we'd useder say we'd do it sometime, an' I'm agoin' to do it now. The rooms, now, they're low—whar they're not to say small, they're low an'—an' old-timey. Thar aint no style to 'em. Them rooms to the Springs, now, they've got style to 'em. An' rooms kin be altered easy enough."

He drank his coffee slowly, set his saucer down and went on with the same serious air of having broached an ordinary subject.

"Goin' to the Springs has sorter started me

off," he said. " Seein' things diff'rent does start
a man off. Casey an' his men'll be here Monday."

" It seems so—sudden," Louisiana said. She
gave a slow, wondering glance at the old smoke-
stained room. " I can hardly fancy it looking any
other way than this. It wont be the same place
at all."

He glanced around, too, with a start. His
glance was hurried and nervous.

" Why, no," he said, " it wont, but—it'll be
stylisher. It'll be kinder onfamil'ar at first, but I
dessay we shall get used to it—an' it'll be stylisher.
An' style—whar thar's young folks, thet's what's
wanted—style."

She was so puzzled by his manner that she sat
regarding him with wonder. But he went on
talking steadily about his plans until the meal
was over. He talked of them when they went
back to the porch together and sat in the moonlight. He scarcely gave her an opportunity to
speak. Once or twice the idea vaguely occurred
to her that for some reason he did not want her
to talk. It was a relief to her only to be called
upon to listen, but still she was puzzled.

" When we git fixed up," he said, " ye kin hev
your friends yere. Thar's them folks, now, as

was yere the other day from the Springs—when we're fixed up ye mought invite 'em—next summer, fur instants. Like as not I shall be away myself an'—ye'd hev room a plenty. Ye wouldn't need me, ye see. An', Lord! how it'd serprise 'em to come an' find ye all fixed."

" I should never ask them," she cried, impetuously. "And—they wouldn't come if I did."

" Mebbe they would," he responded, gravely, " if ye was fixed up."

" I don't want them," she said, passionately. " Let them keep their place. I don't want them."

" Don't ye," he said, in his quiet voice. " Don't ye, Louisianny ? "

And he seemed to sink into a reverie and did not speak again for quite a long time.

5

CHAPTER XI.

A RUSTY NAIL.

ON Monday Casey and his men came. Louisiana and her father were at breakfast when they struck their first blow at the end of the house which was to be renovated first.

The old man, hearing it, started violently—so violently that he almost upset the coffee at his elbow.

He laughed a tremulous sort of laugh.

"Why, I'm narvous!" he said. "Now, jest to think o' me a-bein' narvous!"

"I suppose," said Louisiana, "I am nervous as well. It made me start too. It had such a strange sound."

"Waal, now," he answered, "come to think on it, it hed—sorter. Seems like it wasn't sca'cely nat'ral. P'r'aps that's it."

Neither of them ate much breakfast, and when the meal was over they went out together to look at the workmen. They were very busy tearing off weather-boarding and wrenching out nails. Louisiana watched them with regretful eyes. In secret she was wishing that the low ceilings and painted walls might remain as they were. She had known them so long.

"I am afraid he is doing it to please me," she thought. "He does not believe me when I say I don't want it altered. He would never have had it done for himself."

Her father had seated himself on a pile of plank. He was rubbing his crossed leg as usual, but his hand trembled slightly.

"I druv them nails in myself," he said. "Ianthy wasn't but nineteen. She'd set yere an' watch me. It was two or three months arter we was married. She was mighty proud on it when it was all done. Little Tom he was born in thet thar room. The rest on 'em was born in the front room, 'n' they all died thar. Ianthy she died thar. I'd useder think I should——"

He stopped and glanced suddenly at Louisiana. He pulled himself up and smiled.

"Ye aint in the notion o' hevin' the cupoly," he said. "We kin hev it as soon as not—'n' seems ter me thar's a heap o' style to 'em."

"Anything that pleases you will please m(
father," she said.

He gave her a mild, cheerful look.

"Ye don't take much int'russ in it yet, do ye ?
he said. "But ye will when it gits along kinde
Lord ! ye'll be as impatient as Ianthy an' me wa
when it gits along."

She tried to think she would, but without ver
much success. She lingered about for a while
and at last went to her own room at the other en
of the house and shut herself in.

Her trunk had been carried upstairs and set i
its old place behind the door. She opened it an
began to drag out the dresses and other adorr
ments she had taken with her to the Spring:
There was the blue muslin. She threw it on th
floor and dropped beside it, half sitting, half knee
ing. She laughed quite savagely.

"I thought it was very nice when I made it,
she said. "I wonder how *she* would like to wea
it ?" She pulled out one thing after another unt
the floor around her was strewn. Then she got u
and left them, and ran to the bed and threw herse
into a chair beside it, hiding her face in the pillow

"Oh, how dull it is, and how lonely !" she saic
"What shall I do ? What shall I do ?"

And while she sobbed she heard the blows upon the boards below.

Before she went down-stairs she replaced the things she had taken from the trunk. She packed them away neatly, and, having done it, turned the key upon them.

"Father," she said, at dinner, "there are some things upstairs I want to send to Cousin Jenny. I have done with them, and I think she'd like to have them."

"Dresses an' things, Louisianny?" he said.

"Yes," she answered. "I shall not need them any more. I—don't care for them."

"Don't——" he began, but stopped short, and, lifting his glass, swallowed the rest of the sentence in a large glass of milk.

"I'll tell Leander to send fer it," he said afterward. "Jenny'll be real sot up, I reckon. Her pappy bein' so onfort'nit, she don't git much."

He ate scarcely more dinner than breakfast, and spent the afternoon in wandering here and there among the workmen. Sometimes he talked to them, and sometimes sat on his pile of plank and watched them in silence. Once, when no one was looking, he stooped down and picked up a rusty nail which had fallen from its place in a piece of board. After holding it in his hand for a little he furtively thrust it into his pocket, and seemed to experience a sense of relief after he had done it.

" Ye don't do nothin' toward helpin' us, Uncle Elbert," said one of the young men. (Every youngster within ten miles knew him as " Uncle Elbert.") " Ye aint as smart as ye was when last ye built, air ye ? "

" No, boys," he answered, " I ain't. Thet's so. I aint as smart, an'," he added, rather hurriedly, " it'd sorter go agin me to holp ye at what ye're doin' now. Not as I don't think it's time it was done, but—it'd sorter go ag'in me."

When Louisiana entered the house-room at dusk, she found him sitting by the fire, his body drooping forward, his head resting listlessly on his hand.

" I've got a touch o' dyspepsy, Louisianny," he said, " an' the knockin' hes kinder giv me a head-ache. I'll go to bed airly."

CHAPTER XII.

" MEBBE."

SHE had been so full of her own sharp pain and humiliation during the first few days that perhaps she had not been so quick to see as she would otherwise have been, but the time soon came when she awakened to a bewildered sense of new and strange trouble. She scarcely knew when it was that she first began to fancy that some change had taken place in her father. It was a change she could not comprehend when she recognized its presence. It was no alteration of his old, slow, quiet faithfulness to her. He had never been so faithfully tender. The first thing which awakened her thought of change was his redoubled tenderness. She found that he watched her constantly, in a patient, anxious way. When they were together she often discovered that he kept his eyes fixed upon her when he thought she was not aware of his gaze. He seemed reluctant to leave her alone, and continually managed to be near her, and yet it grew upon her at last that the old, homely good-fellowship between them had somehow been broken in upon, and existed no longer. It was not that he loved her any less—she was sure of that ; but she had lost something, without knowing when or how she had lost it, or even exactly what it was.   But his anxiety to please her grew day by day.   He hurried the men who were at work upon the house.

" Louisianny, she'll enjoy it when it's done," he said to them.   " Hurry up, boys, an' do yer plum best."

She had been at home about two weeks when he began to drive over to the nearest depot every day at " train time."   It was about three miles distant, and he went over for several days in his spring wagon.   At first he said nothing of his reason for making the journey, but one morning, as he stood at his horses' heads, he said to Louisiana, without turning to look at her, and affecting to be very busy with some portion of the harness :

" I've ben expectin' of some things fer a day or so, an' they haint come.   I wasn't sure when I oughter to look fer 'em—mebbe I've ben lookin' too soon—fer they haint come yet."

" Where were they to come from ? " she asked.

" From—from New York City."

" From New York ? " she echoed, trying to show an interest. " I did not know you sent there, father."

" I haint never done it afore," he answered. " These yere things—mebbe they'll come to-day, an' then ye'll see 'em."

She asked no further questions, fancying that he had been buying some adornments for the new rooms which were to be a surprise for her. After he had gone away she thought a little sadly of his kindness to her, and her unworthiness of it. At noon he came back and brought his prize with him.

He drove up slowly with it behind him in the wagon—a large, shining, new trunk—quite as big and ponderous as any she had seen at the Springs.

He got down and came up to her as she stood on the porch. He put his hand on her shoulder.

" I'll hev 'em took in an' ye kin look at 'em," he said. " It's some new things ye was a-needin'."

She began to guess dimly at what he meant, but she followed the trunk into the house without speaking. When they set it down she stood near while her father fumbled for the key and

5*

found it, turned it in the lock and threw back the lid.

" They're some things ye was a-needin'," he said. " I hope ye'll like 'em, honey."

She did not know what it was in his voice, or his face, or his simple manner that moved her so, but she did not look at what he had brought at all—she ran to him and caught his arm, dropped her face on it, and burst into tears.

" Father—father !" she cried. " Oh, father !"

" Look at 'em, Louisianny," he persisted, gently, " an' see if they suit ye. Thar aint no reason to cry, honey."

The words checked her and made her feel uncertain and bewildered again. She stopped crying and looked up at him, wondering if her emotion troubled him, but he did not meet her eye, and only seemed anxious that she should see what he had brought.

" I didn't tell ye all I hed in my mind when I went to the Springs," he said. " I hed a notion I'd like to see fer myself how things was. I knowed ye'd hev an idee thet ye couldn't ask me fer the kind o' things ye wanted, an' I knowed *I* knowed nothin' about what they was, so I ses to myself, ' I'll go an' stay a day an' watch and find out.' An' I went, an' I found out. Thar

was a young woman thar as was dressed purtier
than any of 'em. An' she was clever an' friendly,
an' I managed it so we got a-talkin'. She hed on
a dress that took my fancy. It was mighty black
an' thick—ye know it was cold after the rains—an'
when we was talkin' I asked her if she mind a-
tellin' me the name of it an' whar she'd bought it.
An' she laughed some, an' said it was velvet, an'
she'd got it to some store in New York City.
An' I asked her if she'd write it down; I'd a little
gal at home I wanted a dress off'n it fer—an' then,
someways, we warmed up, an' I ses to her, 'She
aint like me. If ye could see her ye'd never guess
we was kin.' She hadn't never seen ye. She
come the night ye left, but when I told her more
about ye, she ses, 'I think I've heern on her. I
heern she was very pretty.' An' I told her what
I'd hed in my mind, an' it seemed like it took her
fancy, an' she told me to get a paper an' pencil
an' she'd tell me what to send fer an' whar to send.
An' I sent fer 'em, an' thar they air."

She could not tell him that they were things not
fit for her to wear. She looked at the rolls of silk
and the laces and feminine extras with a bewildered feeling.

"They are beautiful things," she said. "I
never thought of having such things for my own."

" Thar's no reason why ye shouldn't hev 'em,"
he said. " I'd oughter hev thought of 'em afore.
Do they suit ye, Louisianny ? "

" I should be very hard to please if they didn't,"
she answered. " They are only too beautiful for
—a girl like me."

" They cayn't be that," he said, gravely. " I
didn't see none no handsomer than you to the
Springs, Louisianny, an' I ses to the lady as writ
it all down fer me, I ses, ' What I want is fer her
to hev what the best on 'em hev. I don't want
nothin' no less than what she'd like to hev if she'd
ben raised in New York or Philadelphy City. Thar
aint no reason why she shouldn't hev it. Out of
eleven she's all that's left, an' she desarves it all.
She's young an' handsome, and she desarves it
all.' "

" What did she say to that ? " Louisiana asked.

He hesitated a moment before answering.

" She looked at me kinder queer fer a minnit,"
he replied at length. " An' then she ses, ' She'd
oughter be a very happy gal,' ses she, ' with such
a father,' an' I ses, ' I 'low she is—mebbe.' "

" Only maybe ? " said the girl, " only maybe,
father ? "

She dropped the roll of silk she had been holding and went to him. She put her hand on his

arm again and shook it a little, laughing in the
same feverish fashion as when she had gone out
to him on the porch on the day of her return.
She had suddenly flushed up, and her eyes shone
as he had seen them then.

"Only maybe," she said. "Why should I
be unhappy? There's no reason. Look at me,
with my fine house and my new things! There
isn't any one happier in the world! There is
nothing left for me to wish for. I have got too
much!"

A new mood seemed to have taken possession
of her all at once. She scarcely gave him a chance
to speak. She drew him to the trunk's side, and
made him stand near while she took the things
out one by one. She exclaimed and laughed over
them as she drew them forth. She held the dress
materials up to her waist and neck to see how the
colors became her; she tried on laces and sacques
and furbelows and the hats which were said to
have come from Paris.

"What will they say when they see me at meeting in them?" she said. "Brother Horner will
forget his sermons. There never were such things
in Bowersville before. I am almost afraid they
will think I am putting on airs."

When she reached a box of long kid gloves at the bottom, she burst into such a shrill laugh that her father was startled. There was a tone of false exhilaration about her which was not what he had expected.

" See ! " she cried, holding one of the longest pairs up, " eighteen buttons ! And cream color ! I can wear them with the cream-colored silk and cashmere at—at a festival ! "

When she had looked at everything, the rag carpet was strewn with her riches,—with fashionable dress materials, with rich and delicate colors, with a hundred feminine and pretty whims.

" How could I help but be happy ? " she said. " I am like a queen. I don't suppose queens have very much more, though we don't know much about queens, do we ? "

She hung round her father's neck and kissed him in a fervent, excited way.

" You good old father ! " she said, " you sweet old father ! "

He took one of her soft, supple hands and held it between both his brown and horny ones.

" Louisianny," he said, " I '*low* to make ye happy ; ef the Lord haint nothin' agin it, I '*low* to do it ! "

He went out after that, and left her alone to set her things to rights ; but when he had gone and closed the door, she did not touch them. She threw herself down flat upon the floor in the midst of them, her slender arms flung out, her eyes wide open and wild and dry.

CHAPTER XIII.

A NEW PLAN.

AT last the day came when the house was fin-
ished and stood big and freshly painted and bare
in the sun. Late one afternoon in the Indian
summer, Casey and his men, having bestowed
their last touches, collected their belongings and
went away, leaving it a lasting monument to their
ability. Inside, instead of the low ceilings, and
painted wooden walls, there were high rooms and
plaster and modern papering ; outside, instead of
the variegated piazza, was a substantial portico.
The whole had been painted a warm gray, and
Casey considered his job a neat one and was proud
of it. When they were all gone Louisiana went
out into the front yard to look at it. She stood
in the grass and leaned against an apple-tree. It
was near sunset, and both trees and grass were
touched with a yellow glow so deep and mellow
that it was almost a golden haze. Now that the

long-continued hammering and sawing was at an end and all traces of its accompaniments removed, the stillness seemed intense. There was not a breath of wind stirring, or the piping of a bird to be heard. The girl clasped her slender arms about the tree's trunk and rested her cheek against the rough bark. She looked up piteously.

"I must try to get used to it," she said. "It is very much nicer—and I must try to get used to it."

But the strangeness of it was very hard on her at first. When she looked at it she had a startled feeling—as if when she had expected to see an old friend she had found herself suddenly face to face with a stranger.

Her father had gone to Bowersville early in the day, and she had been expecting his return for an hour or so. She left her place by the tree at length and went to the fence to watch for his coming down the road. But she waited in vain so long that she got tired again and wandered back to the house and around to the back to where a new barn and stable had been built, painted and ornamented in accordance with the most novel designs. There was no other such barn or stable in the country, and their fame was already wide-spread and of an enviable nature.

As she approached these buildings **Louisiana** glanced up and uttered an exclamation. Her father was sitting upon the door-sill of the barn, and his horse was turned loose to graze upon the grass before him.

" Father," the girl cried, " I have been waiting for you. I thought you had not come."

" I've been yere a right smart while, Louisianny," he answered. " Ye wasn't 'round when I come, an' so ye didn't see me, I reckon."

He was pale, and spoke at first heavily and as if with an effort, but almost instantly he brightened.

" I've jest ben a-settin' yere a-steddyin'," he said. " A man wants to see it a few times an' take it sorter gradual afore he kin do it jestice. A-lookin' at it from yere, now," with a wide sweep of his hand toward the improvements, " ye kin see how much style thar is to it. Seems to me thet the—the mountains now, they look better. It— waal it kinder sets 'em off—it kinder sets 'em off."

" It is very much prettier," she answered.

" Lord, yes! Thar aint no comparison. I was jest a-settin' thinkin' thet any one thet'd seed it as it was afore they'd not know it. Ianthy, fer instants—Ianthy *she* wouldn't sca'cely know it was home—thar's so much style to it."

He suddenly stopped and rested against the door-lintel. He was pale again, though he kept up a stout air of good cheer.

"Lord!" he said, after a little pause, "it's a heap stylisher!"

Presently he bent down and picked up a twig which lay on the ground at his feet. He began to strip the leaves from it with careful slowness, and he kept his eyes fixed on it as he went on talking.

"Ye'll never guess who I've ben a-talkin' to to-day, an' what I've ben talkin' to 'em about."

She put her hand on his knee caressingly.

"Tell me, father," she said.

He laughed a jerky, high-pitched laugh.

"I've ben talkin' to Jedge Powers," he said. "He's up yere from Howelsville, a-runnin' fer senator. He's sot his mind on makin' it, too, an' he was a-tellin' me what his principles was. He —he's got a heap o' principles. An' he told me his wife an' family was a-goin' to Europe. He was mighty sosherble—an' he said they was a-goin' to Europe."

He had stripped the last leaf from the twig and had begun upon the bark. Just at this juncture it slipped from his hand and fell on the ground. He bent down again to pick it up.

" Louisianny," he said, " how—would ye like to go to Europe ? "

She started back amazed, but she could not catch even a glimpse of his face, he was so busy with the twig.

" I go to Europe—I ! " she said. " I don't—I never thought of it. It is not people like us who go to Europe, father."

" Louisianny," he said, hurriedly, " what's agin it ? Thar aint nothin'—nothin' ! It come in my mind when Powers was a-tellin' me. I ses to my-self, ' Why, here's the very thing fer Louisianny ! Travel an' furrin langwidges an' new ways o' doin'. It's what she'd oughter hed long ago.' An' Powers he went on a-talkin' right while I was a-steddyin, an' he ses : ' Whar's that pretty darter o' yourn thet we was so took with when we passed through Hamilton last summer ? Why,' ses he,—he ses it hisself, Louisianny,—' why don't ye send her to Europe ? Let her go with my wife. She'll take care of her.' An' I stopped him right thar. ' Do ye mean it, Jedge ? ' I ses. ' Yes,' ses he. ' Why not ? My wife an' daughter hev talked about her many a time, an' said how they'd like to see her agin. Send her,' ses he. ' You're a rich man, an' ye kin afford it, Squire, if ye will.' An' I ses, ' So I kin ef she'd like to go, an' what's more, I'm a-goin' to ask her ef she would—fer thar aint noth-in' agin it—nothin'.' "

He paused for a moment and turned to look at her.

" Thet's what I was steddyin' about mostly, Louisianny," he said, " when I set yere afore ye come."

She had been sitting beside him, and she sprang to her feet and stood before him.

" Father," she cried, " are you tired of me ? "

" Tired of ye, Louisianny ? " he repeated. " Tired of ye ? "

She flung out her hand with a wild gesture and burst into tears.

" Are you tired of me ? " she said again. " Don't you love me any more ? Don't you want me as you used to ? Could you do without me for months and months and know I was far away and couldn't come to you ? No, you couldn't. You couldn't. I know that, though something—I don't know what—has come between us, and I feel it every minute, and most when you are kindest. Is there nothing in the way of my going away—nothing ? Think again."

" Louisianny," he answered, " I cayn't think of nothin'—thet's partic'lar."

She slipped down on her knee and threw herself

on his breast, clinging to him with all her young strength.

"Are *you* nothing?" she cried. "Is all your love nothing? Are all your beautiful, good thoughts for my happiness 'nothing'? Is your loneliness nothing? Shall I leave you here to live by yourself in the new home which is strange to you—after you have given up the old one you knew and loved for me? Oh! what has made you think I have no heart, and no soul, and nothing to be grateful with? Have I ever been bad and cruel and hard to you that you can think it?"

She poured forth her love and grief and tender reproach on his breast with such innocent fervor that he could scarcely bear it. His eyes were wet too, and his furrowed, sunburnt cheeks, and his breath came short and fast while he held her close in his arms.

"Honey," he said, just as he had often spoken to her when she had been a little child, "Louisi-anny, honey, no! No, never! I never hed a thought agin ye, not in my bottermost heart. Did ye think it? Lord, no! Thar aint nothin' ye've never done in yer life that was meant to hurt or go agin me. Ye never did go agin me. Ye aint like me, honey; ye're kinder finer. Ye was borned so. I seed it when ye was in yer cradle. I've said it to Ianthy (an' sence ye're growed up I've said it more). Thar's things ye'd oughter hev thet's diff'rent from what most of us wants—it's through you a-bein' so much finer. Ye mustn't be so tender-hearted, honey, ye mustn't."

She clung more closely to him and cried afresh, though more softly.

" Nothing shall take me away from you," she said, " ever again. I went away once, and it would have been better if I had stayed at home. The people did not want me. They meant to be good to me, and they liked me, but—they hurt me without knowing it, and it would have been better if I had stayed here. *You* don't make me feel ashamed, and sad, and bitter. *You* love me just as I am, and you would love me if I knew even less, and was more simple. Let me stay with you ! Let us stay together always—always —always ! "

He let her cry her fill, holding her pretty head tenderly and soothing her as best he could. Somehow he looked a little brighter himself, and not quite so pale as he had done when she found him sitting alone trying to do the new house " jestice."

When at length they went in to supper it was

almost dusk, and he had his arm still around her. He did not let her go until they sat down at the table, and then she brought her chair quite close to his, and while he ate looked at him often with her soft, wet eyes.

CHAPTER XIV.

CONFESSIONS.

THEY had a long, quiet evening together afterward. They sat before the fire, and Louisiana drew her low seat near him so that she could rest her head upon his knee.

"It's almost like old times," she said. "Let us pretend I never went away and that everything is as it used to be."

"Would ye like it to be thataway, Louisianny?" he asked.

She was going to say "Yes," but she remembered the changes he had made to please her, and she turned her face and kissed the hand her cheek rested against.

"You mustn't fancy I don't think the new house is beautiful," she said. "It isn't that I mean. What I would like to bring back is—is the feeling I used to have. That is all—nothing but the old feeling. And people can't always have the same

6

feelings, can they ? Things change so as we get older."

He looked at the crackling fire very hard for a minute.

"Thet's so," he said. "Thet's so. Things changes in gin'ral, an' feelin's, now, they're cur'us. Thar's things as kin be altered an' things as cayn't —an' feelin's they cayn't. They're cur'us. Ef ye hurt 'em, now, thar's money ; it aint nowhar —it don't do no good. Thar aint nothin' ye kin buy as 'll set 'em straight. Ef—fer instants— money could buy back them feelin's of yourn— them as ye'd like to hev back—how ready an' willin' I'd be to trade fer' em ! Lord ! how ready an' willin' ! But it wont do it. Thar's whar it is. When they're gone a body hez to larn to git along without 'em."

And they sat silent again for some time, listening to the snapping of the dry wood burning in the great fire-place.

When they spoke next it was of a different subject.

"Ef ye aint a-goin' to Europe—" the old man began.

" And I'm not, father," Louisiana put in.

" Ef ye aint, we must set to work fixin' up right away. This mornin' I was a-layin' out to myself to let it stay tell ye come back an' then hev it all ready fer ye—cheers an' tables—an' sophias—an' merrors—an'—ile paintin's. I laid out to do it slow, Louisianny, and take time, an' steddy a heap, an' to take advice from them es knows, afore I traded ary time. I 'lowed it'd be a heap better to take advice from them es knowed. Brown, es owns the Springs, I 'lowed to hev asked him, now,—he's used to furnishin' up an' knows whar to trade an' what to trade fer. The paintin's, now—I've heern it takes a heap o' experience to pick 'em, an' I aint hed no experience. I 'low I shouldn't know a good un when I seen it. Now, them picters as was in the parlor—ye know more than I do, I dessay,—now, them picters," he said, a little uncertainly, " was they to say good, or—or only about middlin' ? "

She hesitated a second.

" Mother was fond of them," she broke out, in a burst of simple feeling.

Remembering how she had stood before the simpering, red-cheeked faces and hated them ; how she had burned with shame before them, she was stricken with a bitter pang of remorse.

" Mother was fond of them," she said.

" Thet's so," he answered, simply. " Thet's so, she was ; an' you a-bein' so soft-hearted an'

tender makes it sorter go agin ye to give in as
they wasn't—what she took 'em fer. But ye see,
thet—though it's nat'ral—it's nat'ral—don't make
'em good or bad, Louisianny, an' Lord! it don't
harm *her*. 'Taint what folks knows or what they
don't know thet makes the good in 'em. Ianthy
she warn't to say 'complished, but I don't see how
she could hev ben no better than she was—nor
more calc'lated to wear well—in the p'int o' reli-
gion. Not hevin' experience in ile paintin's aint
what'd hurt her, nor make us think no less of her.
It wouldn't hev hurt her when she was livin', an'
Lord! she's past it now—she's past it, Ianthy is."

He talked a good deal about his plans and of
the things he meant to buy. He was quite eager
in his questioning of her and showed such lavish-
ness as went to her heart.

" I want to leave ye well fixed," he said.

" Leave me ? " she echoed.

He made a hurried effort to soften the words.

" I'd oughtn't to said it," he said. " It was
kinder keerless. Thet thar—it's a long way off
—mebbe—an' I'd oughtn't to hev said it. It's a
way old folks hev—but it's a bad way. Things
git to seem sorter near to 'em—an' ordinary."

The whole day had been to Louisiana a slow
approach to a climax. Sometimes when her father

talked she could scarcely bear to look at his face as the firelight shone on it.

So, when she had bidden him good-night at last and walked to the door leaving him standing upon the hearth watching her as she moved away, she turned round suddenly and faced him again, with her hand upon the latch.

"Father," she cried, "I want to tell you—I want to tell you——"

"What?" he said. "What, Louisianny?"

She put her hand to her side and leaned against the door—a slender, piteous figure.

"Don't look at me kindly," she said. "I don't deserve it. I deserve nothing. I have been ashamed——"

He stopped her, putting up his shaking hand and turning pale.

"Don't say nothin' as ye'll be sorry fer when ye feel better, Louisianny," he said. "Don't git carried away by yer feelin's into sayin' nothin' es is hard on yerself. Don't ye do it, Louisianny. Thar aint no need fer it, honey. Yer kinder wrought up, now, an' ye cayn't do yerself jestice."

But she would not be restrained.

"I *must* tell you," she said. "It has been on my heart too long. I ought never to have gone away. Everybody was different from us—and

had new ways. I think they laughed at me, and
it made me bad. I began to ponder over things
until at last I hated myself and everything, and
was ashamed that I had been content. When I
told you I wanted to play a joke on the people
who came here, it was not true. I wanted them
to go away without knowing that this was **my**
home. It was only a queer place, to be laughed
at, to them, and I was ashamed of it, and bitter
and angry. When they went into the parlor they
laughed at it and at the pictures, and everything in
it, and I stood by with my cheeks burning. When
I saw a strange woman in the kitchen it flashed
into my mind that I had no need to tell them
that all these things that they laughed at had been
round me all my life. They were not sneering at
them—it was worse than that—they were only interested and amused and curious, and were not
afraid to let me see. The—gentleman had been
led by his sister to think I came from some city.
He thought I was—was prettty and educated,—
his equal, and I knew how amazed he would be
and how he would say he could not believe that
I had lived here, and wonder at me and talk me
over. And I could not bear it. I only wanted
him to go away without knowing, **and never,**
never see me again !"

Remembering the pain and fever and humiliation of the past, and of that dreadful day above all, she burst into sobbing.

"You did not think I was that bad, did you?" she said. "But I was! I was!"

"Louisianny," he said, huskily, "come yere. Thar aint no need fer ye to blame yerself thataway. Yer kinder wrought up."

"Don't be kind to me!" she said. "Don't! I want to tell you all—every word! I was so bad and proud and angry that I meant to carry it out to the end, and tried to—only I was not quite bad enough for one thing, father—I was not bad enough to be ashamed of *you*, or to bear to sit by and see them cast a slight upon you. They didn't mean it for a slight—it was only their clever way of looking at things—but *I* loved you. You were all I had left, and I knew you were better than they were a thousand times! Did they think I would give your warm, good heart—your kind, faithful heart —for all they had learned, or for all they could ever learn? It killed me to see and hear them! And it seemed as if I was on fire. And I told them the truth—that you were *my* father and that I loved you and was proud of you—that I might be ashamed of myself and all the rest, but not of you—never of you—for I wasn't worthy to kiss your feet!"

For one moment her father watched her, his lips parted and trembling. It seemed as if he meant to try to speak, but could not. Then his eyes fell with an humble, bewildered, questioning glance upon his feet, encased in their large, substantial brogans—the feet she had said she was not worthy to kiss. What he saw in them to touch him so it would be hard to tell—for he broke down utterly, put out his hand, groping to feel for his chair, fell into it with head bowed on his arm, and burst into sobbing too.

She left her self-imposed exile in an instant, ran to him, and knelt down to lean against him.

"Oh!" she cried, "have I broken your heart? Have I broken your heart? Will God ever forgive me? I don't ask you to forgive me, father, for I don't deserve it."

At first he could not speak, but he put his arm round her and drew her head up to his breast—and, with all the love and tenderness he had lavished upon her all her life, she had never known such love and tenderness as he expressed in this one movement.

"Louisianny," he said, brokenly, when he had found his voice, "it's you as should be a-forgivin' me."

"I!" she exclaimed.

He held her in his trembling **arm so** close **that** she felt his heart quivering.

"To think," he almost whispered, "as I should **not hev ben doin'** ye jestice! To think as I didn't **know** ye well enough to **do ye jestice!** To think yer **own father,** thet's knowed ye all **yer life,** could **hev give in to its bein'** likely as ye wasn't—what **he'd allers thought, an'** what **yer** mother 'd thought, an' what **ye was, honey."**

"I don't——" she began falteringly.

"It's me as oughter **be** a-standin' agin the door," he said. "It's me! I knowed every word of the first part of **what ye've told me,** Louisianny. **I've been so sot on ye thet I've got** into a kinder **noticin'** way with ye, an' I guessed it **out.** I seen it in yer **face when** ye stood thar tryin' to laugh on the porch while them people **was a-waitin'.** 'Twa'n't no nat'ral gal's laugh ye laughed, and when ye thought I wasn't a-noticin' I was a-noticin' an' a-thinkin' all the time. But I seen more than was thar, honey, an' I didn't do ye jestice—an' I've ben punished fer it. It come agin me like a slungshot. I ses to myself, 'She's ashamed o' *me!* It's *me* she's ashamed of—an' she wants to pass me off fer **a** stranger!'"

The girl drew off **from** him a little **and** looked up into his face wonderingly.

6*

"You thought that!" she said. "And never told me—and humored me, and——"

"I'd oughter knowed ye better," he said; "but I've suffered fer it, Louisianny. I ses to myself, 'All the years thet we've ben sot on each other an' nussed each other through our little sick spells, an' keered fer each other, hes gone fer nothin'. She wants to pass me off fer a stranger.' Not that I blamed ye, honey. Lord! I knowed the difference betwixt us! *I*'d knowed it long afore you did. But somehow it warn't eggsakly what I looked fer an' it was kinder hard on me right at the start. An' then the folks went away an' ye didn't go with 'em, an' thar was somethin' workin' on ye as I knowed ye wasn't ready to tell me about. An' I sot an' steddied it over an' watched ye, an' I prayed some, an' I laid wake nights a-steddyin'. An' I made up my mind thet es I'd ben the cause o' trouble to ye I'd oughter try an' sorter balance the thing. I allers 'lowed parents hed a duty to their child'en. An' I ses, 'Thar's some things thet kin be altered an' some thet cayn't. Let's alter them es kin!'"

She remembered the words well, and now she saw clearly the dreadful pain they had expressed; they cut her to her soul.

"Oh! father," she cried. "How could you?"

"I'd oughter knowed ye better, Louisianny,"
he repeated. "But I didn't. I ses, 'What
money an' steddyin' an' watchin'll do fer her to
make up, shell be done. I'll try to make up
fer the wrong I've did her onwillin'ly—onwillin'ly.' An' I went to the Springs an' I watched
an' steddied thar, an' I come home an' I watched
an' steddied thar—an' I hed the house fixed, an'
I laid out to let ye go to Europe—though what
I'd heern o' the habits o' the people, an' the bri-
gands an' sich, went powerful agin me makin' up
my mind easy. An' I never lost sight nary minnit o' what I'd laid out fer to do—but I wasn't
doin' ye jestice an' didn't suffer no more than I'd
oughter. An' when ye stood up thar agen the
door, honey, with yer tears a-streamin' an' yer
eyes a-shinin', an' told me what ye'd felt an' what
ye'd said about—wa'l," (delicately) "about thet
thar as ye thought ye wasn't worthy to do, it set
my blood a-tremblin' in my veins—an' my heart
a-shakin' in my side, an' me a-goin' all over—an'
I was struck all of a heap, an' knowed thet the
Lord hed ben better to me than I thought, an'—
an' even when I was fondest on ye, an' proudest
on ye, I hadn't done ye no sort o' jestice in the
world—an' never could!"

There was no danger of their misunderstanding

each other again. When they were calmer they talked their trouble over simply and confidingly, holding nothing back.

" When ye told me, Louisianny," said her father, " that ye wanted nothin' but me, it kinder went agin me more than all the rest, fer I thinks, ses I to myself, ' It aint true, an' she must be a-gettin' sorter hardened to it, or she'd never said it. It seemed like it was kinder onnecessary. Lord! the onjestice I was a-doin' ye!"

They bade each other good-night again, at last.

" Fer ye're a-lookin' pale," he said. " An' I've been kinder out o' sorts myself these last two or three weeks. My dyspepsy's bin back on me agin an' thet thar pain in my side's bin a-workin' on me. We must take keer o' ourselves, bein' es thar's on'y us two, an' we're so sot on each other."

He went to the door with her and said his last words to her there.

" I'm glad it come to-night," he said, in a grateful tone. " Lord! how glad I am it come to-night! S'posin' somethin' hed happened to ary one of us an' the other hed ben left not a-knowin' how it was. I'm glad it didn't last no longer, Louisianny."

And so they parted for the night.

CHAPTER XV.

"IANTHY!"

IT was later than usual when Louisiana awakened in the morning. She awakened suddenly and found herself listening to the singing of a bird on the tree near her window. Its singing was so loud and shrill that it overpowered her and aroused her to a consciousness of fatigue and exhaustion.

It seemed to her at first that no one was stirring in the house below, but after a few minutes she heard some one talking in her father's room—talking rapidly in monotonous tone.

"I wonder who it is," she said, and lay back upon her pillow, feeling tired out and bewildered between the bird's shrill song and the strange voice.

And then she heard heavy feet on the stairs and listened to them nervously until they reached her door and the door was pushed open unceremoniously.

The negro woman Nancy thrust her head into the room.

"Miss Louisianny, honey," she said. "Ye aint up yet?"

"No."

"Ye'd better *git* up, honey—an' come down stairs."

But the girl made no movement.

"Why?" she asked, listlessly.

"Yer pappy, honey—he's sorter cur'us. He don't seem to be right well. He didn't seem to be quite at hisself when I went to light his fire. He——"

Louisiana sat upright in bed, her great coil of black hair tumbling over one shoulder and making her look even paler than she was.

"Father!" she said. "He was quite well late last night. It was after midnight when we went to bed, and he was well then."

The woman began to fumble uneasily at the latch.

"Don't ye git skeered, chile," she said. "Mebbe 'taint nothin'—but seemed to me like—like he didn't know me."

Louisiana was out of bed, standing upon the floor and dressing hurriedly.

"He was well last night," she said, piteously.

"Only a few hours ago. He was well and talked to me and——"

She stopped suddenly to listen to the voice down-stairs—a new and terrible thought flashing upon her.

"Who is with him?" she asked. "Who is talking to him?"

"Thar aint no one with him," was the answer. "He's by hisself, honey."

Louisiana was buttoning her wrapper at the throat. Such a tremor fell upon her that she could not finish what she was doing. She left the button unfastened and pushed past Nancy and ran swiftly down the stairs, the woman following her.

The door of her father's room stood open and the fire Nancy had lighted burned and crackled merrily. Mr. Rogers was lying high upon his pillow, watching the blaze. His face was flushed and he had one hand upon his chest. He turned his eyes slowly upon Louisiana as she entered and for a second or so regarded her wonderingly. Then a change came upon him, his face lighted up—it seemed as if he saw all at once who had come to him.

"Ianthy!" he said. "I didn't sca'cely know ye! Ye've bin gone so long! Whar hev ye bin?"

But even then she could not realize the truth. It was so short a time since he had bidden her good-night and kissed her at the door.

"Father!" she cried. "It is Louisiana! Father, look at me!"

But he was looking at her, and yet he only smiled again.

"It's bin such a long time, Ianthy," he said. "Sometimes I've thought ye wouldn't never come back at all."

And when she fell upon her knees at the bed-side, with a desolate cry of terror and anguish, he did not seem to hear it at all, but lay fondling her bent head and smiling still, and saying happily:

"Lord! I *am* glad to see ye!"

When the doctor came—he was a mountaineer like the rest of them, a rough good-natured fellow who had "read a course" with somebody and "'tended lectures in Cincinnatty"—he could tell her easily enough what the trouble was.

"Pneumony," he said. "And pretty bad at that. He haint hed no health fer a right smart while. He haint never got over thet spell he hed last winter. This yere change in the weather's what's done it. He was a-complainin' to me the

other day about thet thar old pain in his chist.
Things hes bin kinder 'cumylatin' on him."

"He does not know me!" said Louisiana.
"He is very ill—he is very ill!"

Doctor Hankins looked at his patient for a moment, dubiously.

"Wa-al, thet's so," he said, at length. "He's
purty bad off—purty bad!"

By night the house was full of visitors and vol-
unteer nurses. The fact that "Uncle Elbert Rogers was down with pneumony, an' Louisianny
thar without a soul anigh her" was enough to
rouse sympathy and curiosity. Aunt 'Mandy,
Aunt Ca'line and Aunt 'Nervy came up one after
the other.

"Louisianny now, she aint nothin' but a young
thing, an' don't know nothin'," they said. "An'
Elbert bein' sich nigh kin, it'd look powerful bad
if we didn't go."

They came in wagons or ricketty buggies and
brought their favorite medicines and liniments
with them in slab-sided, enamel-cloth valises.
They took the patient under their charge, applied
their nostrums and when they were not busy
seemed to enjoy talking his symptoms over in low
tones. They were very good to Louisiana, reliev-
ing her of every responsibility in spite of herself,

and shaking their heads at each other pityingly when her back was turned.

"She never give him no trouble," they said. "She's got thet to hold to. An' they was powerful sot on her, both him an' Ianthy. I've heern 'em say she allus was kinder tender an' easy to manage."

Their husbands came to " sit up " with them at night, and sat by the fire talking about their crops and the elections, and expectorating with regularity into the ashes. They tried to persuade Louisiana to go to bed, but she would not go.

"Let me sit by him, if there is nothing else I can do," she said. "If he should come to himself for a minute he would know me if I was near him."

In his delirium he seemed to have gone back to a time before her existence—the time when he was a young man and there was no one in the new house he had built, but himself and "Ianthy." Sometimes he fancied himself sitting by the fire on a winter's night and congratulating himself upon being there.

"Jest to think," he would say in a quiet, speculative voice, "that two year ago I didn't know ye—an' thar ye air, a-sittin' sewin', and the fire a-cracklin', an' the house all fixed. This yere's what I call solid comfort, Ianthy—jest solid comfort!"

Once he wakened suddenly from a sleep and finding Louisiana bending over him, drew her face down and kissed her.

"I didn't know ye was so nigh, Ianthy," he whispered. "Lord! jest to think yer allers nigh an' thar cayn't nothin' separate us."

The desolateness of so living a life outside his, was so terrible to the poor child who loved him, that at times she could not bear to remain in the room, but would go out into the yard and ramble about aimless and heart-broken, looking back now and then at the new, strange house, with a wild pang.

"There will be nothing left if he leaves me," she said. "There will be nothing."

And then she would hurry back, panting, and sit by him again, her eyes fastened upon his unconscious face, watching its every shade of expression and change.

"She'll take it mighty hard," she heard Aunt Ca'line whisper one day, "ef——"

And she put her hands to her ears and buried her face in the pillow, that she might not hear the rest.

CHAPTER XVI.

"DON'T DO NO ONE A ONJESTICE."

HE was not ill very long. Toward the end of the second week the house was always full of visitors who came to sympathize and inquire and prescribe, and who, in many cases, came from their farms miles away attracted by the news that "Uncle Elbert Rogers" was "mighty bad off." They came on horseback and in wagons or buggies—men in homespun, and women in sunbonnets—and they hitched their horses at the fence and came into the house with an awkwardly subdued air, and stood in silence by the sick bed for a few minutes, and then rambled towards the hearth and talked in spectral whispers.

"The old man's purty low," they always said, "he's purty low." And then they added among themselves that he had "allers bin mighty clever, an' a good neighbor."

When she heard them speak of him in this

manner, Louisiana knew what it meant. She
never left the room again after the first day that
they spoke so, and came in bodies to look at him,
and turn away and say that he had been good
to them. The men never spoke to her after their
first nod of greeting, and the women but rarely,
but they often glanced hurriedly askance at her as
she sat or stood by the sick man's pillow. Somehow none of them had felt as if they were on very
familiar terms with her, though they all spoke in
a friendly way of her as being " a mighty purty,
still, kind o' a harmless young critter." They
thought, when they saw her pallor and the anguish
in her eyes, that she was "takin' it powerful
hard, an' no wonder," but they knew nothing of
her desperate loneliness and terror.

" Uncle Elbert he'll leave a plenty," they said
in undertones. " She'll be well pervided fer,
will Louisianny."

And they watched over their charge and nursed
him faithfully, feeling not a little sad themselves
as they remembered his simple good nature and
neighborliness and the kindly prayers for which
he had been noted in " meetin'."

On the last day of the second week the doctor
held a consultation with Aunt 'Nervy and Aunt
Ca'line on the front porch before he went away,

and when they re-entered the room they spoke in whispers even lower than before and moved about stealthily. The doctor himself rode away slowly and stopped at a house or so on the wayside, where he had no patients, to tell the inhabitants what he had told the head nurses.

"We couldn't hev expected him to stay allers," he said, "but we'll miss him mightily. He haint a enemy in the county—nary one!"

That afternoon when the sun was setting, the sick man wakened from a long, deep sleep. The first thing he saw was the bright pale-yellow of a tree out in the yard, which had changed color since he had seen it last. It was a golden tree now as it stood in the sun, its leaves rustling in a faint, chill wind. The next thing, he knew that there were people in the room who sat silent and all looked at him with kindly, even reverent, eyes. Then he turned a little and saw his child, who bent towards him with dilated eyes and trembling, parted lips. A strange, vague memory of weary pain and dragging, uncertain days and nights came to him and he knew, and yet felt no fear.

"Louisianny!" he said.

He could only speak in a whisper and tremulously. Those who sat about him hushed their very breath.

"Lay yer head—on the piller—nigh me," he said.

She laid it down and put her hand in his. The great tears were streaming down her face, but she said not a word.

" I haint got long—honey," he faltered. " The Lord—He'll keer—fer ye."

Then for a few minutes he lay breathing faintly, but with his eyes open and smiling as they rested on the golden foliage of the tree.

"How yaller—it is!" he whispered. "Like gold. Ianthy was powerful—sot on it. It—kinder beckons."

It seemed as if he could not move his eyes from it, and the pause that followed was so long that Louisiana could bear it no longer, and she lifted her head and kissed him.

" Father!" she cried. " Say something to *me!* Say something to *me!* "

It drew him back and he looked up into her eyes as she bent over him.

" Ye'll be happy—" he said, " afore long. I kinder—know. Lord! how I've—loved ye, honey—an' ye've desarved it—all. Don't ye—do no one—a onjestice."

And then as she dropped her white face upon the pillow again he saw her no longer—nor the people, nor the room, but lay quite still with parted lips and eyes wide open, smiling still at the golden tree waving and beckoning in the wind.

This he saw last of all, and seemed still to see even when some one came silently, though with tears, and laid a hand upon his eyes.

CHAPTER XVII.

A LEAF.

THERE was a sunny old grave-yard half a mile from the town, where the people of Bowersville laid their dead under the long grass and tangle of wild-creeping vines, and the whole country-side gathered there when they lowered the old man into his place at his wife's side. His neighbors sang his funeral hymn and performed the last offices for him with kindly hands, and when they turned away and left him there was not a man or woman of them who did not feel that they had lost a friend.

They were very good to Louisiana. Aunt 'Nervy and Aunt Ca'line deserted their families that they might stay with her until all was over, doing their best to give her comfort. It was Aunt 'Nervy who first thought of sending for the girl cousin to whom the trunkful of clothes had been given.

7

" Le's send for Leander's Jenny, Ca'line," she said. " Mebbe it'd help her some to hev a gal nigh her. Gals kinder onderstands each other, an' Jenny was allus powerful fond o' Lowizyanny."

So Jenny was sent for and came. From her lowly position as one of the fifteen in an " onfort'-nit" family she had adored and looked up to Louisiana all her life. All the brightest days in her experience had been spent at Uncle Elbert's with her favorite cousin. But there was no bright-ness about the house now. When she arrived and was sent upstairs to the pretty new room Louisi-ana occupied she found the girl lying upon the bed. She looked white and slender in her black dress; her hands were folded palm to palm under her cheek, and her eyes were wide open.

Jenny ran to her and knelt at her side. She kissed her and began to cry.

" Oh ! " she sobbed, "somehow I didn't ever think I should come here and not find Uncle Elbert. It don't seem right—it makes it like a strange place."

Then Louisiana broke into sobs, too.

" It *is* a strange place ! " she cried—" a strange place—a strange place ! Oh, if one old room was left—just one that I could go into and not feel so lonely ! "

But she had no sooner said it than she checked herself.

" Oh, I oughtn't to say that ! " she cried. " I wont say it. He did it all for *me*, and I didn't deserve it."

" Yes, you did," said Jenny, fondling her. " He was always saying what a good child you had been—and that you had never given him any trouble."

" That was because he was so good," said Louisiana. " No one else in the whole world was so good. And now he is gone, and I can never make him know how grateful I was and how I loved him."

" He did know," said Jenny.

" No," returned Louisiana. " It would have taken a long, long life to make him know all I felt, and now when I look back it seems as if we had been together such a little while. Oh ! I thought the last night we talked that there was a long life before us—that I should be old before he left me, and we should have had all those years together."

After the return from the grave-yard there was a prolonged discussion held among the heads of the different branches of the family. They gathered at one end of the back porch and talked of

Louisiana, who sat before the log fire in her room upstairs.

"She aint in the notion o' leavin' the place," said Aunt 'Nervy. "She cried powerful when I mentioned it to her, an' wouldn't hear to it. She says over an' over ag'in 'Let me stay in the home he made for me, Aunt Ca'line.' I reckon she's a kind o' notion Elbert 'lowed fur her to be yere when he was gone."

"Wa-al now," said Uncle Leander, "I reckon he did. He talked a heap on it when he was in a talkin' way. He's said to me 'I want things to be jest as she'd enjoy 'em most—when she's sorter lonesome, es she will be, mebbe.' Seemed like he hed it in his mind es he warnt long fur this world. Don't let us cross her in nothin'. *He* never did. He was powerful tender on her, was Elbert."

"I seed Marthy Lureny Nance this mornin'," put in Aunt Ca'line, "an' I told her to come up an' kinder overlook things. She haint with no one now, an' I dessay she'd like to stay an' keep house."

"I don't see nothin' ag'in it," commented Uncle Steve, "if Louisianny don't. She's a settled woman, an's bin married, an'haint no family to pester her sence Nance is dead."

"She was allers the through-goin' kind," said Aunt 'Nervy. "Things 'll be well looked to— an' she thought a heap o' Elbert. They was raised together."

"S'pos'n ye was to go in an' speak to Louisianny," suggested Uncle Steve.

Louisiana, being spoken to, was very tractable. She was willing to do anything asked of her but go away.

"I should be very glad to have Mrs. Nance here, Aunt Minerva," she said. "She was always very kind, and father liked her. It won't be like having a strange face near me. Please tell her I want her to come and that I hope she will try to feel as if she was at home."

So Marthy Lureny Nance came, and was formally installed in her position. She was a tall, strongly-built woman, with blue eyes, black hair, and thick black eyebrows. She wore, when she arrived, her best alpaca gown and a starched and frilled blue sun-bonnet. When she presented herself to Louisiana she sat down before her, removed this sun-bonnet with a scientific flap and hung it on the back of her chair.

"Ye look mighty peak-ed, Louisianny," she said. "Mighty peak-ed."

" I don't feel very well," Louisiana answered, " but I suppose I shall be better after a while."

" Ye're takin' it powerful hard, Louisianny," said Mrs. Nance, " an' I don't blame ye. I aint gwine to pester ye a-talkin'. I jest come to say I 'lowed to do my plum best by ye, an' ax ye whether ye liked hop yeast or salt risin' ? "

At the end of the week Louisiana and Mrs. Nance were left to themselves. Aunt 'Nervy and Aunt Ca'line and the rest had returned to their respective homes, even Jenny had gone back to Bowersville where she boarded with a relation and went to school.

The days after this seemed so long to Louisiana that she often wondered how she lived through them. In the first passion of her sorrow she had not known how they passed, but now that all was silence and order in the house, and she was alone, she had nothing to do but to count the hours. There was no work for her, no one came in and out for whom she might invent some little labor of love ; there was no one to watch for, no one to think of. She used to sit for hours at her window watching the leaves change their color day by day, and at last flutter down upon the grass at the least stir of wind.

Once she went out and picked up one of these leaves and taking it back to her room, shut it up in a book.

"Everything has happened to me since the day it was first a leaf," she said. "I have lived just as long as a leaf. That isn't long."

When the trees were bare, she one day remembered the books she had sent for when at the Springs, and she went to the place where she had put them, brought them out and tried to feel interested in them again.

"I might learn a great deal," she said, "if I persevered. I have so much time."

But she had not read many pages before the tears began to roll down her cheeks.

"If he had lived," she said, "I might have read them to him and it would have pleased him so. I might have done it often if I had thought less about myself. He would have learned, too. He thought he was slow, but he would have learned, too, in a little while, and he would have been so proud."

She was very like her father in the simple tenderness of her nature. She grieved with the hopeless passion of a child for the unconscious wrong she had done.

It was as she sat trying to fix her mind upon

these books that there came to her the first thought
of a plan which was afterwards of some vague comfort to her.   She had all the things which had fur-
nished the old parlor taken into one of the unused
rooms—the chairs and tables, the carpet, the or-
naments and pictures.   She spent a day in plac-
ing everything as she remembered it, doing all
without letting any one assist her.   After it was
arranged she left the room, and locked the door
taking the key with her.

"No one shall go in but myself," she said.   "It
belongs to me more than all the rest."

"I never knowed her to do nothin' notionate
but thet," remarked Mrs. Nance, in speaking of
it afterwards.   "She's mighty still, an' sits an'
grieves a heap, but she aint never notionate.
Thet *was* kinder notionate fer a gal to do.   She
sets store on 'em 'cos they was her pappy's an' her
ma's, I reckon.   It cayn't be nothin' else, fur they
aint to say stylish, though they was allers good
solid-appearin' things.   The picters was the on'y
things es was showy."

"She's mighty pale an' slender sence her pappy
died," said the listener.

"Wa-al, yes, she's kinder peak-ed," admitted
Mrs. Nance.   "She's kinder peak-ed, but she'll
git over it.   Young folks allers does."

But she did not get over it as soon as Mrs. Nance had expected, in view of her youth. The days seemed longer and lonelier to her as the winter advanced, though they were really so much shorter, and she had at last been able to read and think of what she read. When the snow was on the ground and she could not wander about the place she grew paler still.

"Louisianny," said Mrs. Nance, coming in upon her one day as she stood at the window, "ye're a-beginnin' to look like ye're Aunt Melissy."

"Am I?" answered Louisiana. "She died when she was young, didn't she?"

"She wasn't but nineteen," grimly. "She hed a kind o' love-scrape, an' when the feller married Emmerline Ruggles she jest give right in. They hed a quarrel, an' he was a sperrity kind o' thing an' merried Emmerline when he was mad. He cut off his nose to spite his face, an' a nice time he hed of it when it was done. Melissy was a pretty gal, but kinder consumpshony, an' she hedn't backbone enough to hold her up. She died eight or nine months after they'd quarreled. Mebbe she'd hev died anyhow, but thet sorter hastened it up. When folks is consumpshony it don't take much to set 'em off."

7*

"I don't think I am 'consumpshony,'" said Louisiana.

"Lord-a-massy, no!" briskly, "an' ye'd best not begin to think it. I wasn't a meanin' thet. Ye've kinder got into a poor way steddyin' 'bout yere pappy, an' it's tellin' on ye. Ye look as if thar wasn't a thing of ye—an' ye don't take no int'russ. Ye'd oughter stir round more."

"I'm going to 'stir round' a little as soon as Jake brings the buggy up," said Louisiana. "I'm going out."

"Whar?"

"Toward town."

For a moment Mrs. Nance looked at her charge steadily, but at length her feelings were too much for her. She had been thinking this matter over for some time.

"Louisianny," she said, "you're a-gwine to the grave-yard, thet's whar ye're a-gwine an' thar aint no sense in it. Young folks hedn't ought to hold on to trouble thataway—'taint nat'ral. They don't gin'rally. Elbert 'd be ag'in it himself ef he knowed—an' I s'pose he does. Like as not him an' Ianthy's a-worryin' about it now, an' Lord knows ef they air it'll spile all their enjoyment. Kingdom come won't be nothin' to 'em if they're oneasy in their minds 'bout ye. Now an' ag'in it's 'peared to me that mebbe harps an' crowns an' the company o' 'postles don't set a body up all in a minnit an' make 'em forgit their flesh an' blood an' nat'ral feelin's teetotally—an' it kinder troubles me to think o' Elbert an' Ianthy worryin' an' not havin' no pleasure. Seems to me ef I was you I'd think it over an' try to cheer up an' take int'russ. Jest think how keerful yer pappy an' ma was on ye an' how sot they was on hevin' ye well an' happy."

Louisiana turned toward her. Her eyes were full of tears.

"Oh!" she whispered, "do you—do you think they know?"

Mrs. Nance was scandalized.

"Know!" she echoed. "Wa-al now, Louisi-anny, ef I didn't know yer raisin', an' thet ye'd been brought up with members all yer life, it'd go ag'in me powerful to hear ye talk thetaway. Ye *know* they know, an' thet they'll take it hard, ef they aint changed mightily, but, changed or not, I guess thar's mighty few sperrits es haint sense enough to see yer a-grievin' more an' longer than's good fur ye."

Louisiana turned to her window again. She rested her forehead against the frame-work and looked out for a little while. But at last she spoke.

"Perhaps you are right," she said. "It is true it would have hurt them when they were here. I think—I'll try to—to be happier."

"It's what'll please 'em best, if ye do, Louisianny," commented Mrs. Nance.

"I'll try," Louisiana answered. "I will go out now—the cold air will do me good, and when I come back you will see that I am—better."

"Wa-al," advised Mrs. Nance, "ef ye go, mind ye put on a plenty—an' don't stay long."

The excellent woman stood on the porch when the buggy was brought up, and having tucked the girl's wraps round her, watched her driven away.

"Mebbe me a-speakin's I did'll help her," she said. "Seems like it kinder teched her an' sot her thinkin'. She was dretfle fond of her pappy an' she was allers a purty peaceable advise-takin' little thing—though she aint so little nuther. She's reel tall an' slim."

CHAPTER XVIII

"HE KNEW THAT I LOVED YOU."

IT was almost dark when the buggy returned. As Jake drove up to the gate he bent forward to look at something.

"Thar's a critter hitched to the fence," he remarked. "'Taint no critter from round yere. I never seen it afore."

Mrs. Nance came out upon the porch to meet them. She was gently excited by an announcement she had to make.

"Louisianny," she said, "thar's a man in the settin'-room. He's a-waitin' to see ye. I asked him ef he hed anything to sell, an' he sed no he hedn't nothin'. He's purty *gen*-teel an' stylish, but not to say showy, an' he's polite sort o' manners."

"Has he been waiting long?" Louisiana asked.

"He's ben thar half a hour, an' I've hed the fire made up sence he come."

Louisiana removed her hat and cloak and gave them to Mrs. Nance. She did it rather slowly, and having done it, crossed the hall to the sitting-room door, opened it and went in.

There was no light in the room but the light of the wood fire, but that was very bright. It was so bright that she had not taken two steps into the room before she saw clearly the face of the man who waited for her.

It was Laurence Ferrol.

She stopped short and her hands fell at her sides. Her heart beat so fast that she could not speak.

His heart beat fast, too, and it beat faster still when he noted her black dress and saw how pale and slight she looked in it. He advanced towards her and taking her hand in both his, led her to a chair.

" I have startled you too much," he said. " Don't make me feel that I was wrong to come. Don't be angry with me."

She let him seat her in the chair and then he stood before her and waited for her to speak.

" It was rather—sudden," she said, " but I am not—angry."

There was a silence of a few seconds, because he was so moved by the new look her face wore that he could not easily command his voice and words.

"Have you been ill?" he asked gently, at last.

He saw that she made an effort to control herself and answer him quietly, but before she spoke she gave up even the effort. She did not try to conceal or wipe away the great tears that fell down her cheeks as she looked up at him.

"No, I have not been ill," she said. "My father is dead."

And as she uttered the last words her voice sank almost into a whisper.

Just for a breath's space they looked at each other and then she turned in her chair, laid her arm on the top of it and her face on her arm, with a simple helpless movement.

"He has been dead three months," she whispered, weeping.

His own eyes were dim as he watched her. He had not heard of this before. He walked to the other end of the room and back again twice. When he neared her the last time he stopped.

"Must I go away?" he asked unsteadily. "I feel as if I had no right here."

But she did not tell him whether he must go or stay.

"If I stay I must tell you why I came and why I could not remain away," he said.

She still drooped against her chair and did not speak, and he drew still nearer to her.

"It does not seem the right time," he said, "but I must tell you even if I go away at once afterwards. I have never been happy an hour since we parted that wretched day. I have never ceased to think of what I had begun to hope for. I felt that it was useless to ask for it then—I feel as if it was useless now, but I must ask for it. Oh!" desperately, "how miserably I am saying it all! How weak it sounds!"

In an instant he was kneeling on one knee at her side and had caught her hand and held it between both his own.

"I'll say the simplest thing," he said. "I love you. Everything is against me, but I love you and I am sure I shall never love another woman."

He clasped her hand close and she did not draw it away.

"Won't you say a word to me?" he asked. "If you only tell me that this is the wrong time and that I must go away now, it will be better than some things you might say."

She raised her face and let him see it.

"No," she said, "it is not that it is the wrong

time. It is a better time than any other, because I am so lonely and my trouble has made my heart softer than it was when I blamed you so. It is not that it is the wrong time, but——"

"Wait a minute," he broke in. "Don't—don't do me an injustice!"

He could not have said anything else so likely to reach her heart. She remembered the last faltering words' she had heard as she bent over the pillow when the sun was shining on the golden tree with the wind waving its branches.

"Don't do no one a onjestice, honey—don't ye—do no one—a onjestice."

"Oh," she cried out, "he told me that I must not—he told me, before he died!"

"What!" said Ferrol. "He told you not to be unjust to *me*?"

"It was you he meant," she answered. "He knew I had been hard to you—and he knew I——"

She cowered down a little and Ferrol folded her in his arms.

"Don't be hard to me again," he whispered. "I have been so unhappy—I love you so tenderly. Did he know that you—speak to me, Louise."

She put her hand upon his shoulder.

"He knew that I loved you," she said, with a little sob.

She was a great favorite among her husband's friends in New York the next year. One of her chief attractions for them was that she was a "new type." They said that of her invariably when they delighted in her and told each other how gentle she was and how simple and sweet. The artists made "studies" of her, and adored her, and were enthusiastic over her beauty; while among the literary ones it was said, again and again, what a foundation she would be for a heroine of the order of those who love and suffer for love's sake and grow more adorable through their pain.

But these, of course, were only the delightful imaginings of art, talked over among themselves, and Louisiana did not hear of them. She was very happy and very busy. There was a gay joke current among them that she was a most tremendous book-worm, and that her literary knowledge was something for weak, ordinary mortals to quail before. The story went, that by some magic process she committed to memory the most appalling works half an hour after they were issued from the press, and that, secretly, Laurence stood very much in awe of her and was constantly afraid of exposing his ignorance in her presence. It was certainly true that she read a great deal, and showed a wonderful aptness and memory, and that Laurence's pride and delight in her were the strongest and tenderest feelings of his heart.

Almost every summer they spent in North Carolina, filling their house with those of their friends who would most enjoy the simple quiet of the life they led. There were numberless pictures painted among them at such times and numberless new " types" discovered.

" But you'd scarcely think," it was said sometimes, "that it is here that Mrs. Laurence is on her native heath."

And though all the rest of the house was open, there was one room into which no one but Laurence and Louisiana ever went—a little room, with strange, ugly furniture in it, and bright-colored lithographs upon the walls.

END.